$b

Happiness was not part of the contract . . .

Jess couldn't repress a shiver when the studded oak doors of the castle gates closed behind them. As she cast a glance at the man behind the wheel of the Jaguar, she had one overwhelming thought.

Trapped. She was trapped.

She gave a hunted look behind her, and her strained eyes met only the unbroken line of impregnable walls. Before her lay the castle itself, really just an imposing manor house. Although the grounds were filled with bright gardens, the formidable ancient gray walls brought home to her, as nothing else could have, just how vulnerable and weak she would be as Max's wife.

She made one fervent vow. *I must not have his child . . .*

SUE PETERS grew up in the idyllic countryside of Warwickshire, England, and began writing romance novels quite by chance. "Have a go," her mother suggested when a national writing contest sponsored by Mills and Boon appeared in the local newspaper. Sue's entry placed second, and a career was born. After completing her first romance novel, she missed the characters so much she started another and another.... Now she's as addicted to writing as she is to gardening, which she often does as she's formulating new plots.

Books by Sue Peters

HARLEQUIN ROMANCE

1975—CLOUDED WATERS
2030—ONE SPECIAL ROSE
2104—PORTRAIT OF PARADISE
2156—LURE OF THE FALCON
2204—ENTRANCE TO THE HARBOUR
2351—SHADOW OF AN EAGLE
2368—CLAWS OF A WILDCAT
2410—MARRIAGE IN HASTE
2423—TUG OF WAR
2471—DANGEROUS RAPTURE
2501—MAN OF TEAK
2583—LIGHTNING STRIKES TWICE
2812—NEVER TOUCH A TIGER
2892—ENTRANCE TO EDEN
2915—CAPTURE A NIGHTINGALE
2938—ONE-WOMAN MAN

UNWILLING WOMAN

Sue Peters

Harlequin Books

TORONTO • NEW YORK • LONDON
AMSTERDAM • PARIS • SYDNEY • HAMBURG
STOCKHOLM • ATHENS • TOKYO • MILAN

Original hardcover edition published in 1989
by Mills & Boon Limited

ISBN 0-373-03018-5

Harlequin Romance first edition November 1989

CHAPTER ONE

'SMILE, Lucy, for goodness' sake. You look so glum, you make me think I'm fitting a dress on a bride sacrifice, instead of a girl who's in love. What's the matter? Don't you like the dress I've designed for you? It isn't too late to change the style to a lower neckline, if you like it better that way.'

There was more than a hint of concern in the look Jess Donaldson cast at her client's fairy-like reflection in the long mirror. The cloud of pale ivory silk, richly appliquéd in handmade lace, the cost of which had evaporated almost the whole of Jess's meagre business capital to date, flowed from the girl's slender figure as if it was moulded to her.

Jess had no qualms about the fit of the gown. She and her client were exactly the same measurements, and she knew, because she had tried it on herself, that the dress fitted like a dream.

The thing which brought the frown to her forehead was the despairing expression on the nineteen-year-old face, which should have looked radiant under the lovely lace veil that covered the neat cap of shining dark hair.

The success of this commission was desperately important to Jess. It was vitally necessary that she recoup the cost of the exotic materials which Lucy had chosen, in order to restore her own slender bank balance. And, too, the success of the wedding gown, and the fabulous trousseau which she had designed especially for the young bride, would, Jess hoped, gain her many more clients from Lucy's exalted social circle, and so set the seal of success on the small business which she had struggled so hard to get off the ground since she had left college.

During their student days, she and Lucy had been on different courses. The younger girl had taken pure domestic science, whereas Jess's own fascination for beautiful materials, and her precocious talent at designing, had led her in other directions.

Her infrequent meetings with Lucy had been of the hail-fellow-well-met variety, among crowds of others at the various student gatherings, which left no room for personal revelations, and the information about Lucy's background had come as a minor bombshell one morning when Jess went shopping with her erstwhile contemporary to choose materials for Lucy's wedding gown, trousseau, and going-away outfit.

The jeans and sweater attired student, whom Jess had known hitherto, had headed straight for the top people's stores, and ordered what took her fancy without even a glance at the price tickets.

'Watch it, you're spending a fortune,' Jess had cautioned, but Lucy had answered carelessly,

'My allowance will cope. Don't worry,' as Jess's expression had still betrayed concern. 'Even if it doesn't, my parents' executors are reasonable about what they call extra necessary expenditure. I don't gain control of my money until I'm twenty-five, but they know that Max won't expect me to walk down the aisle in an off-the-peg wedding dress from one of the local department stores.'

'Max being your fiancé, I presume?'

'Max being my fiancé, and the Earl of Blythe, no less. Although he doesn't use his title unless he has to. He prefers to use his family name, and simply be known as

Max Beaumont. He owns Blythe Castle. It lies some way north of the River Wye. You might know it.'

Jess did not. The lovely hinterland was still a dream which she hoped to explore one day, when she had time to spare. She had replied drily, 'A castle will be quite a contrast to rooms on the college campus.' Lucy's fiancé must be supremely self-assured to be able to ignore his title, and rely upon being simply himself, she had thought.

'Mmm.' Lucy's reply had been non-committal, and Jess had wondered if she would perhaps prefer a flat in London to living in the country. But that was Lucy's business, and she had let it pass, and turned the conversation back to the task in hand, that of matching lace to silk and veiling.

She viewed the made up results now, with satisfaction. 'These are a perfect match. You'll look a dream when you walk down the aisle.'

'You must come to the wedding. It'll help, if you're there.'

It was an odd way of wording an invitation, but Jess dismissed the thought for another, more personal one.

'It's short notice to make myself something to wear,' she demurred. 'I've been so busy making clothes for other people since I left college, I haven't had time to make any for myself.'

If she went as a guest to Lucy's wedding, she would be obliged to buy a wedding present as well, she realised with dismay, which would eat still further into her depleted resources, on top of having to purchase yet more material for her own outfit, and spend time she could not afford in making it up.

Mentally, Jess assessed her own sparse wardrobe. None of her clothes were suitable for a wedding at a castle. In her two brief years in business so far, all her time and

money had been ploughed back into her work, and she
still made do with the same few outfits which had seen
her through her student days. While good, they were
mostly by now well worn, except for one or two which
she kept for special occasions, and none of them wedding
attire.

It had been hard grind since she left the coveted course
at the famous London college, and the scholarship grant
which had brought her there from her high school in
New Zealand had ended along with the course.

Now that her student days were behind her, it was
Jess's ambition to make a name for herself as a dress
designer before she eventually returned to her native
country, successful, and with sufficient funds to set up
a home and a business there as well.

To achieve her dream, she knew that she would have
to work for every penny herself. The small amount she
had inherited from the grandparents who had raised her
was almost gone by the time her college course was finished, and, with the sturdy resolution of her pioneering
ancestors, the then twenty-one-year-old Jess spent the
rest of it on a brand new sewing machine, and set up in
business.

With no family to fall back on, she clear-sightedly
faced the fact that she must first work in order to eat,
and during the initial year her normally slight frame grew
even more slender, and hollows developed in her fine-
boned cheeks, a sure barometer of the arduous hours
she spent in her small bedsitter, translating her own in-
spired designs into dreamlike reality for her clients.

At first she had concentrated on wedding clothes, for
the simple reason that her numerous friends and ac-
quaintances among the ex-students of her college year
were all of marriageable age, and provided her with a
much-needed clientèle, and they came to her because her

charges were moderate. Word of her talent was beginning to spread, however, and recently she had netted several orders for ball gowns and special occasion outfits from older clients, to whom cost was not of paramount importance.

Lucy, it appeared, came into this fortunate category, and her social standing could open the way to an up-market clientèle which Jess might otherwise have spent years in trying to attract. It was the sort of break she had dreamed about, but never imagined might come her way.

It was obvious from Lucy's downcast expression, however, that something was worrying her, and Jess's frown deepened when the girl turned to her and begged tensely, 'I don't mind what you wear, so long as you come. Wear slacks and a sweater, for all I care, but promise me you'll turn up. I don't think I can go through with it otherwise.'

'Hey, what's this you're saying?' Jess drew off the lace veil and folded it carefully before commencing to slide the bridal gown off the young shoulders.

To her dismay, she saw that they were shaking uncontrollably. Hurriedly she slipped the dress on to a hanger and hooked it safely out of the way on the picture rail, before turning back to the younger girl.

'Cheer up, Lucy. It'll be all right on the day, you'll see.'

'No, it won't.' The words choked out on a sob.

'You've got a bad attack of wedding nerves, that's all.'

It was not the first case of its kind Jess had experienced with her clients, but with the gentle-natured and rather timid nineteen-year-old, the nerves seemed to be manifesting themselves in a rather more exaggerated form than usual, she thought compassionately, as she helped the unresisting girl into her street clothes.

'Every bride has last-minute doubts,' she encouraged. 'They all wonder if they're doing the right thing. And when they get to the altar, all their doubts vanish. You won't need any more fittings, after today...'

'That's just it,' Lucy burst out. 'I don't want to go to the altar. At least, not with Max.'

'But...' Jess stared in consternation as Lucy buried her face in her hands and burst into tears, and sobbed disjointedly,

'Max and I don't love one another enough. He's a lot older than me. He must be at least thirty.'

Compassion made Jess bite back a smile at her client's immature view of her fiancé's early prime, but Lucy rushed on.

'Ever since my parents died, Max has kept a sort of older-brotherly eye on me. We're distantly related, and I suppose he felt some sort of responsibility towards me. He proposed when I was staying at Blythe Castle last summer, and it seemed the most natural thing in the world that we should get married. But now I know that it was the most dreadful mistake.'

Her sobs increased in violence. Jess thrust a bunch of tissues into the girl's shaking fingers, and followed it up with a cup of hot, strong coffee, ready perking on the stove.

'Sit down, and calm down, and get it off your chest. Talking about it might make you feel better.'

This was more than just pre-wedding nerves, but at least it explained the oddly worded invitation, Jess thought, as Lucy obediently mopped her streaming eyes, and, slightly restored by a gulp of the inky brew, went on more coherently, 'Nothing can make me feel any worse than I do now. If only Max had proposed to Nina Vaughan instead.'

'Nina Vaughan?' Jess's raised eyebrows asked the question, and Lucy explained,

'The Vaughans bought The Grange when the old colonel died. It's in the same village as the castle. They're business people with pots of money, and they've set their minds on getting a title for their daughter. Nina would go to any lengths to capture Max. She uses every excuse she can think of to come to the castle, and she hangs round Max like a Christmas tree decoration. I used to hate her for it, until I met David Glover again. That was when I realised that what Max and I felt for one another just wasn't enough. You remember David Glover, from college?'

Jess nodded. She had liked the little she had seen of the clean-cut, eager young engineering student. 'I haven't seen him since I graduated.'

'Neither had I, until a few months ago. We met quite by chance, and started going out together. David landed a good job as soon as he left college, Jess, and he's already been offered a promotion.'

Animation brightened Lucy's face, and her eyes shone with the expression that should have lit them, and had not, when she had tried on the wedding dress.

'And?' Jess prompted.

'The job David's been offered is abroad, and he wants me to go with him. As his wife, of course,' Lucy added hastily. 'We both know it will be hard going for the first few years. We won't have much money until David's made his way, but that won't matter. We'll have one another.'

'You'll be giving up a good deal,' Jess felt obliged to point out. 'The sort of life you've obviously been used to. Wealth, and now a title.'

'That won't matter. Titles and wealth don't matter. David can win both for us eventually, if he wants them. All I want is him. Can't you understand, Jess? I love David. I'm fond of Max, too, of course, but in a completely different way.'

Jess understood, and her respect for her client deepened. 'So, what's the problem? Keep the wedding gown, and swap the bridegroom,' she said briskly. More seriously she added, 'You'll have to tell your fiancé. You can't marry one man when you love another. Call the wedding off, or at least postpone it until you're absolutely clear in your own mind what you want to do.'

'I know what I want to do. I want to marry David. Oh, Jess, it's all such a tangle,' Lucy wailed.

'It's one you'll have to unravel before you can start knitting it up again to the pattern you want,' Jess said practically.

'Max is going to be absolutely furious. Everything's arranged. He's fixed up a huge champagne reception at the castle, and it's only two weeks away.'

'If the wedding was only two days away, I still say you should cancel it. You can't sacrifice your entire future, and the future of the man you love, just for the sake of feeding a lot of people who don't need it with a lot of posh nosh. If your fiancé won't agree to cancel the wedding, and he tries to make you go through with it, simply elope and leave him to eat through the wedding breakfast himself.'

Jess strove to introduce a lighter note as she saw Lucy through the door, and her efforts were rewarded by the beginnings of a smile as the younger girl said gratefully, 'You've given me Dutch courage. I'll go down to Blythe Castle tonight and get it over with.'

Jess shut the door on Lucy's retreating figure, and returned thoughtfully to her room. It was only when she caught sight of the wedding dress hanging from the picture rail that her own aspect of the unhappy situation struck her.

If Lucy really did elope, she, Jess, would be left with the clothes she had made on her hands. She had practically cleaned out her entire bank account in order to pay for the exotic materials, and it would mean building up her already meagre funds all over again if Lucy did not use the clothes, and, more importantly, pay for them.

She knew of no one else who would be likely to buy such an expensive wardrobe. Her fellow ex-students were all more or less in the same position as herself, in the current jargon 'upwardly mobile', but still penurious; although they might cast envious eyes on the garments, they would never be able to afford them. The few older and more affluent clients she had attracted up to now all mirrored their larger bank balances, and the clothes, however desirable, would not fit them.

And, too, with Lucy's going she would lose access to any future clients from the girl's social circle, on whom Jess had built such hopes of achieving her future dreams. Lucy's broken engagement might well set back her own plans by several years.

Jess sighed, and began to leaf tissue paper in between layers of silk and lace. She hoped Lucy would not become so wrapped up in her own problems that she would forget to keep in touch with what she intended to do about them.

It might not occur to the well-connected girl just how parlous someone else's financial situation could be, when she herself did not have to worry unduly about such a mundane thing as money. In vain during the two days of blank silence which followed their conversation, Jess tried to reassure herself that, whichever man eventually won Lucy's hand, the girl would still want her wedding clothes.

She did not take seriously her own suggestion that Lucy should elope if her present fiancé proved to be difficult. Such a drastic step would be entirely contrary to the younger girl's rather timorous nature.

Nevertheless, as the hours ticked by without the hoped-for telephone call, Jess's consternation increased, and, when the doorbell rang on the second morning after Lucy's departure, she flew to answer it.

'Lucy?' She ground to a halt as she flung open the door.

It was not Lucy who stood on the mat; but her client's previous description of the tall stranger, whose broad shoulders seemed to fill the small vestibule, had been accurate enough to dispense with the need for an introduction. Jess's visitor was the young and startlingly handsome Earl of Blythe. Or, as he preferred to be known, Max Beaumont. And it was clear that he had been, and still was, just as furious at his fiancée's fickle behaviour as Lucy had fearfully predicted. Worse, his scowl suggested that, for some obscure reason, he blamed Jess for it.

'I want an explanation from you,' he snapped, and pushed his way through the door without waiting for an invitation.

Perforce Jess had to step backwards to avoid being run down. A detached part of her mind wondered how Max Beaumont could be so sure of who she was. Perhaps Lucy had described her with equal clarity. But beech-brown, wavy hair, with deep coppery tints in it, and eyes that made wide pools of apprehensive hazel in a finely boned face, was a description that could apply to any one of a thousand girls.

Her visitor, however, seemed to have no doubts as to her identity. Jess surmised that he probably never did have any doubts about anything which he himself decided upon, and blinked under the gimlet scrutiny of eyes that were as grey as northern skies. The look they bent upon Jess was about as friendly as a northern blizzard, and her visitor's temper seemed to match the blackness of his hair as he swung on Jess in the minute bedsitter, and demanded,

'What right have you got to tell Lucy to take off and elope in this irresponsible manner? Have you got any idea of the trouble you've caused?'

'Eloped? *Lucy?*'

'You heard me.'

Jess had heard him clearly enough, but she could not believe the evidence of her own ears. It was preposterous to imagine that the gentle-natured Lucy had really plucked up enough courage to elope. It was totally out of character.

But love could change even the most timid character. Lucy was a woman in love, and women in love were wont to break free from the chrysalis of their old inhibitions, and emerge as brilliant and surprisingly brave butterflies.

This particular butterfly had evidently spread her wings and flown, acting on Jess's purely flippant suggestion in a way that she could never have envisaged when she made it.

And Lucy's wrathful fiancé, or ex-fiancé as he must be by now, was calling Jess to account for his betrothed's defection. Her chin came up, and she faced him bravely.

'I didn't tell Lucy to elope. I only meant it as a joke. I never imagined she would act on it.'

'*Joke?*' he thundered, in a voice that made the pot plants rattle on their saucers, and Jess's nerves along with them. '*Joke?* Do you call it a joke, to cancel a wedding of this size at the eleventh hour? I've got more than enough on my plate as it is, without being saddled with the task of sending written apologies to over four hundred guests, to say nothing of being landed with returning a host of unwanted wedding presents. And as to the cost of the reception, and the ball that was to follow it afterwards...'

Words seemed to fail him, but not for long. He ignored Jess's faint, 'Four hundred guests?' and swept on grimly, 'That isn't counting the honeymoon.'

Jess's stomach muscles contracted into a tight knot as the catalogue lengthened, but she fought back spiritedly. 'It's no use shouting at me. I'm not responsible if Lucy decides to opt out of marrying a man she doesn't love.'

'She had for ever to make up her mind. She's known me all her life. And she was happy with our engagement until she got talking to you.'

'That's probably the trouble. Knowing you all her life, I mean. She probably wanted a change.'

'She hasn't known this other man for five minutes. He's nothing more than a chance acquaintance from college. A nobody.'

The scorn in his voice sharpened the tone of her reply. 'He's got a name. It's David Glover. And what if they did meet at college? That makes him something more than just a chance acquaintance. In any case——' underneath her practical exterior Jess was a pure romantic at heart, although she would stoutly deny such a thing to any but her closest friends '—in any case, if they'd only just bumped into one another in the street, and something clicked between them, that's enough. You may not believe it, but love at first sight does happen. And when it does, they're the lucky ones.'

Max Beaumont did not seem to Jess as if he would ever allow himself to be taken by storm in such a manner. Love, if and when it happened to him, would be very strictly under his own control. Cupid would perforce have to direct his arrows where the master of Blythe Castle willed, and woe betide the mischievous archer, Jess thought wryly, if he should be so misguided as not to hit the desired bull's-eye first time.

'She was happy enough, until you interfered.'

'Lucy didn't think so, or she wouldn't have cut and run. It's better for her to break off the engagement now, rather than risk having a divorce later. Surely you can see that? David's going to marry her, for goodness' sake, he isn't going to shack up with her.'

She ignored his low growl of anger, and rushed on before he could speak. 'As for me interfering, Lucy's quite old enough to know her own mind about who she wants to spend the rest of her life with. She doesn't need anyone else to spell it out for her.'

'Your influence tipped the scales.'

'So, I'm a bad influence. Well, let me tell you something, my Lord.' Goaded by the injustice of his accusation, Jess sketched her visitor a sarcastic curtsy, and had the satisfaction of seeing dull colour rise under the healthy outdoor tan of his cheeks. 'Let me tell you something. The bother of a cancelled wedding is as nothing to the misery of Lucy going through with the ceremony, knowing that she is marrying the wrong man. I'd influence anyone against doing such a crazy thing. And as for your hundreds of guests, if you're so busy that you can't manage to let them know the wedding's off, just let them come as arranged, and hold the reception anyway. Have yourself a party,' she cried recklessly. 'If you're so bothered about calling off the ceremony in the church itself, why not go the whole way, and find another bride? You won't need to cancel anything at all, then.'

The moment she saw his colour recede, Jess knew she had gone too far. With a move so swift that it evaded her eye, Max Beaumont's hand shot out, his fingers closed like steel bands around her wrist, and he jerked her to him.

'That's an excellent suggestion,' he gritted. 'You'll do nicely as a substitute bride.'

His lips clamped down across her own, stifling her startled gasp. The pressure of them was implacable, denying her movement to struggle free, and punishing her for Lucy's defection, as well as for her own temerity in daring to defy him.

Jess was gasping for breath, and furious, when he finally let her go.

'Beast!'

Angrily she wiped a hand across her lips in a frantic gesture that tried without success to extinguish the fire which scorched their soft fullness with the imprint of his kiss.

She was aware of Max Beaumont's grey eyes watching her, piercing the jumbled confusion of her thoughts that had reduced her normal calm composure to a chaos that left her dazed and shaking.

She dragged air into her straining lungs with a harsh rasping sound. The grey eyes were mesmerising her. Drowning her. Something undecipherable flared in their fathomless depths, akin to the fire which had burned her lips, and which, unless she acted quickly, might return and scorch her again.

Jess grasped at anger as a sword with which to strike out and defend herself.

'I wouldn't marry you if you were the last man left on earth. You must be joking, if you think...'

'Go ahead and laugh,' he interrupted her harshly. 'You're good at making jokes. You've only got yourself to blame if you have to pay for the consequences of this one.'

'You can't possibly be serious.' Jess's mind boggled at the mere suggestion.

'I was never more so.' The steely grey eyes, with the curious, flaring light in their depths that seemed to grow stronger by the minute, rooted Jess to the floor, making her feel as helpless as a butterfly caught on a pin. 'A wedding has been arranged, and one way or another I intend to see that it takes place. I won't be made the laughing-stock of the county by a couple of irresponsible, conniving girls calling the whole thing off at the last minute.'

Raggedly Jess wondered how anyone would dare to laugh at Max Beaumont and expect to get away with it. She had never felt less like laughing in her life before.

With a feeling of numb horror, it dawned upon her that her tormentor did, indeed, mean exactly what he said. And arrogantly expected her to fall into line with his preposterous suggestion without raising a single peep of protest.

'You're crazy!' she gasped. 'You can't force me to marry you.'

Who did this man think he was? Jess felt as if she was being enmeshed in a web of unreality, with Max Beaumont as the spider in the middle. A devastatingly handsome spider, who conceded grimly, 'Not *force* you. I can offer a compelling inducement to make you agree.'

'Such as you as the bridegroom, I suppose? I'll never agree.' Jess's laugh was shrill. The man's conceit was unbelievable.

'No, not me.' The flare in the grey eyes grew in intensity, making Jess blink under the brilliant light.

'Then what . . . ?'

'My inducement is of a more commercial nature. Either you agree to marry me, or I'll wreck your business. Lucy told me what a struggle you'd had to build it up from scratch. OK, so you've got it off the ground.' His voice held a grudging respect for her achievement so far. 'But to keep it airborne, you need decent commissions in order to get your name known in the right quarters, and attract more business of the same calibre. One word from me around town about what you've done, and the whole of London will turn its back on you.'

And she would have to turn her back on her dreams. He swept aside Jess's faint, 'You're mad. You wouldn't dare,' with a confident,

'On the contrary, I'm very sane, and if you try to defy me, you'll very soon discover exactly what I will dare. You've got talent. You must have, to be able to produce clothes like that.' His eyes swept over the wedding dress and going-away outfits which hung from the picture rail, and on which Jess had been working when his knock on the door had interrupted her. 'But even your talent can't exist on run-of-the-mill orders from an area like this. The large chain-stores can undercut any price you will be able to quote.'

His voice lashed her, and Jess bit her lip. She knew he spoke the truth, however unpalatable. Her special talents needed the freedom to design top-of-the-range clothing, and through Lucy she already had her foot on the first rung of the ladder. But her footing on that rung was insecure, and Max Beaumont had the ability to topple her from it with the ease of flicking a fly off a wall, perhaps never to rise again.

And he knew it. He was wealthy and titled, and who knew how far his influence might spread?

Surreptitiously assessing the clothes he himself wore, Jess reckoned that he would have the power to ruin her chances not only in London, but probably the rest of the UK, and even on the Continent as well. His circle of friends, and people like the Vaughans who aspired to call themselves his friends because of his social position, and would therefore slavishly follow his every word, could be limitless.

Jess's silence was eloquent of the tumult of her thoughts, and reading them with uncanny accuracy Max Beaumont swept on ruthlessly. 'You can use the wedding dress and the trousseau yourself. You look to be about the same size as Lucy.' His eyes raked Jess with a cool, assessing glance that made her skin prickle, and then swivelled briefly back to where the wedding dress hung from the picture rail. 'I'm sure the clothes you made for my ex-fiancée will look even more becoming on you. I'll leave you to think over what I've said.'

It was Max Beaumont's turn now to return a mocking bow, and before Jess could gather her wits together sufficiently to reply, he was gone.

She was dreaming. It was a nightmare. She would wake up soon and make herself a strong cup of coffee, and laugh about the whole fantastic episode.

But the sound of firm, masculine footsteps demolishing the length of the hall in two long strides, and the street door emphasising their owner's departure with a decided slam, held the conviction of waking reality.

The noise jolted Jess's paralysed muscles into action, and she stumbled to the window in time to see her visitor open the driving door of a sleek maroon Jaguar car parked at the paving edge.

As she pressed her nose to the glass, he looked up and back, and held her transfixed for a long moment with a hard, compelling stare, before he bent and jack-knifed his long length into the driving seat, and steered the big car smoothly away into the busy stream of city traffic.

Jess turned away from the window and groped for a chair with a hand that shook, in order to relieve her protesting knees of a suddenly unendurable burden.

This madness must not go any further. She refused to marry any man, even an earl, simply in order to salve his pride, and avoid cancelling his wedding. That it was his pride, and not his heart, which was wounded, Jess did not doubt for one moment. No human heart could possibly exist under such a granite exterior.

By now Lucy was presumably well out of reach of his wrath, so he was turning the full force of his fury upon herself, Jess, and seeking cruelly to punish her for Lucy's defection, hurting her as a balm for his own wounds. Jess's own innate sense of fairness cried out at the injustice of what he was threatening to do.

If his aim was merely to try to frighten her, she had to admit that he had succeeded beyond his wildest dreams. She was frankly terrified. She did not know which prospect alarmed her more, marrying the arrogant, self-assured Lord Blythe of Blythe Castle, or seeing the results of all her striving since she left college set at naught, with any chance of rebuilding her hard-won gains destroyed by the vengeance of an embittered man. The latter alternative filled her with dread, while the former filled her with a strange kind of excitement that frightened her even more.

Briefly she toyed with the idea of returning to New Zealand and starting all over again in her native country, where surely Max Beaumont's influence could not reach. But, no matter how she juggled with the figures on her

latest bank statement, the total told her uncompromis-
ingly that, since funding Lucy's extravagant choice of
materials for the wedding finery and trousseau, what was
left was insufficient to cover even the cheapest fare.

During the long, sleepless hours of the night which
followed, Jess managed to eventually convince herself
that, having achieved his objective in thoroughly frightening her, Max Beaumont would be content to leave it
at that. People often made threats in a fit of anger which
they had no real intention of carrying out, and when he
had arrived on her humble doorstep that morning, there
was no doubt that the noble earl had been very, very
angry indeed.

By the next morning, however, his anger must surely
have cooled, and upon reflection he would realise what
an impossible position he was putting himself in, as well
as her. Jess was proud of her name, but honest enough
to admit that her lineage hardly qualified her for a
mention in Debrett, let alone putting her in the marriage
stakes to a member of the peerage, and in the cool light
of day Max Beaumont must surely come to the same
conclusion.

Jess did not make the mistake of assuming that he
had followed her own example, and spent the entire night
awake, agonising over the possible consequences of his
infamous suggestion. By the time he arrived at his
breakfast coffee, however, sanity must surely prevail, and
tell him that it was better to cancel the wedding arrangements rather than blackmail an unwilling bride to accompany him to the altar.

The fallacy of her argument was made abundantly
clear to her before her own breakfast-time coffee had
time to cool in its cup. An early summons to the street
door, which Jess assumed to be the postman with some

material samples for which she was waiting, turned out
to be Max Beaumont.

'You again,' she stammered, aghast.

'Who did you expect? Your steady boyfriend?' His
keen glance raked her dismayed face.

'I don't have a steady...' Jess stopped. Why did she
have to tell him that? If she had pretended to a steady
boyfriend, with an engagement ring in the offing, it
would have given her a strong lever with which to extricate herself from the impossible situation into which
this even more impossible man had driven her.

His next remark demonstrated his contempt of strong
levers. He shrugged, carelessly. 'That makes things easier
all round if I don't have to clear the decks of unwanted
suitors first, before we get married.'

Jess stared at him, stunned. 'You can't mean that you
really intend to go through with this nonsense?'

'It isn't nonsense, I assure you. And in case you still
feel inclined to argue, what I've brought with me should
convince you that I mean business.'

'Marriage shouldn't be a business contract.'

In spite of herself, Jess's voice cracked. All the cher-
ished dreams of her own warm heart revolted against
such a cold-blooded arrangement, and humiliatingly she
knew that her distress must betray her deepest feelings
on her all too revealingly mobile features.

'Marriage should be for love,' she blurted out.

Briefly a strange expression crossed the stern, tanned
face looking down at her, and then it was gone, and its
owner answered crisply, 'As you said, those are the lucky
ones. But you do have a choice. I'll give you until the
end of the week to make up your mind.'

His choice was no choice at all. Jess watched disbelievingly as he placed a small ring box on the table in
front of her, and flicked open the lid with a long index

finger. Inside, on a bed of soft velvet, lay a ring of such beauty that it rounded her eyes.

Previously she had seen such jewels only through the plate-glass windows of the more exclusive West End jewellers. A blood red ruby winked at her from the centre of a cluster of diamonds of flawless clarity, and, confused, she thought, how did he know that the ruby is my birthstone?

He could not have known. It was impossible. And yet, in her brief experience of Max Beaumont, she had discovered that he had a flair for the impossible.

With a numb feeling of inevitability, Jess watched the long, tanned fingers, with the smoothly rounded filbert nails, reach into the ring box, and pluck the shiny jewel from off its resting place.

'Try it on to see if I've guessed the size right.'

His look held her, mesmerising her. Jess tried to tear her gaze away, and found to her dismay that she could not. It clung to the lean, hard face above her with the frozen stare of a trapped wild creature, staring at its own doom.

'Try it on.'

'No!'

He reached down and took her left hand, and his touch stung like a white-hot branding iron. His brand, upon her shrinking flesh, that clenched her fingers into a tight ball to prevent him from slipping the ring on to her finger.

'No!'

Stung back to life, Jess tried unsuccessfully to jerk her hand free as she faced him with dilated eyes.

'I don't want to try it on. I don't want...'

'As you wish.'

He carefully slotted the ring back into its box, but he still retained his hold upon her hand.

'You said you'd give me until the end of the week,' she persisted desperately. Perhaps by the end of the week, a miracle might happen. Perhaps...

'Perhaps this will help you to reach the right decision.'

The right one for him, or for her? His implacable hold upon her was an answer in itself.

His closeness was overpowering. His arms were like two steel bands round her, forcing her resisting body against him, while his lips moved across her mouth with a sensuous pressure that aroused her every nerve-end into a tingling awareness of him.

With cynical expertise he teased her tight lips apart, demanding a response from them that Jess was determined not to give, but to her dismay she felt her own lips begin to purse under his in a response of their own that she was totally unable to control.

Slight though the movement was, he felt it, and his kiss changed and deepened, holding her mouth for a long, agonising minute before he held her away from him, and mocked her with a mirthless smile of triumph.

'Will that help you to make up your mind? I'll call back on Saturday morning, and you can let me know your decision then.'

Saturday morning. It was already Tuesday, and, faced with a choice between bankruptcy or a loveless marriage to a total stranger, her decision had to be a foregone conclusion.

Throughout the rest of that day, Jess's mind twisted and turned in a vain attempt to find a solution, but by bedtime none had presented itself.

Her independent spirit longed to throw the ring back in Max Beaumont's haughty face, and tell him in no uncertain terms to keep it, and hang the consequences.

But if she did, and he carried out his threat to ruin her business, what then? Jess did not doubt that he was quite capable of doing just that, and the prospect appalled her. A word here and there would be all that it would need. In Max Beaumont's tightly knit social circle, word would soon spread, and any prospective clients would be frightened off for fear of offending the eligible young earl.

Visions of having to sell her precious sewing machine in order to pay her rent made Jess feel physically sick. Without her machine she would not only be penniless, but she would be denied the means of earning even a modest living. The alternative was equally unthinkable.

That evening, Liz Wallace interrupted her distraught thoughts in one of her rare telephone calls from New Zealand. Liz was the one close friend with whom Jess had kept in touch since she had left home, and even across the width of the world her friend was quick to detect that all was not well with her listener.

'You don't sound your usual chirpy self. What's up?' Liz demanded, characteristically forthright.

'Everything,' Jess replied grimly, and wasted no time in pouring out her troubles.

'There's only one piece of advice I can give you,' Liz offered when she came to a halt.

'Tell me,' Jess begged urgently.

She groaned out loud when Liz replied briskly, 'Marry the man, of course. Where else would you find a millionaire with a title? Must go, Jess, there's the pips. Write and let me know how you get on.'

The phone went dead. Jess slid the receiver back on to its rest, and collapsed limply on to a chair.

Max Beaumont had won, just as he knew he would. There was no way out of the situation. Unless he relented, she would be obliged to go through with the cer-

emony, and marry him. Become a substitute bride to a
complete stranger, who was prepared to resort to
blackmail to serve his own ends, and whom she
thoroughly and heartily detested.

When he arrived to get her answer early on the following Saturday morning, he showed not the slightest
sign of relenting.

During the intervening days, Jess's nerves had
tightened until they twanged like fiddle strings at each
ring of the doorbell. Countless measures of escape had
burned through her fevered mind as she'd tossed and
turned throughout each sleepless night, only to be rejected out of hand.

Should she run away? Simply disappear, without trace,
where Max Beaumont could not find her? But to do so
she would be obliged to carry all her worldly possessions
with her, an impossibility when the major possession
consisted of a large and extremely heavy sewing machine.

Should she stay and fight him? What will you use for
money to live on, when he's wrecked your business?
common sense jeered.

The only alternative was to throw herself on his mercy
and beg, and her sturdy pride revolted at the thought of
humbling herself before the arrogant Earl of Blythe.

His dark, hawklike face held no hint of mercy when
he faced her for the third time in her minute bedsitter
on the fateful Saturday morning, and demanded curtly,
'Well? What have you decided?'

Third time lucky, but not for Jess. 'My business is all
I've got to live on.'

She ground out the words through clenched teeth.
Words of capitulation. They burned like corrosive acid
on her tongue, and she hated the smile of triumph that
returned to his lips, but did nothing to warm the steely
grey of his eyes, as he reached out and picked up the

ring box from the table where it had remained un-
touched since his last visit.

He snapped open the lid with the same sure flick of
his finger as before, and removed the ring, and his eyes
reflected the hard glint of the stones as he took the short
step necessary to bring him up close against Jess.

'Have you tried this on yet, to see if it will fit
you?'

She shook her head numbly. 'Lord Blythe...' she burst
out, and in spite of her resolution not to beg her eyes
held a desperate appeal.

'Call me Max. As we're going to be married in five
days' time, it will look strange if you insist upon treating
me so formally.'

'Five days? It's impossible. Even you can't force things
through so quickly. There are such things as banns to
be read, and ...'

'I've already taken out a special licence.'

He had been so sure of her that he had pre-empted
her answer. Jess's wrath rose at his arrogance.

'There are other things to be considered. You can't
simply substitute one bride for another, like the wave of
a magic wand.'

'For instance?'

'There has to be somebody to give me away.'

She was stalling for time, and it was fast running out.
She was not being given away, she was being hijacked,
and Jess choked back threatening tears as Max swept
aside her objection with a casual, 'My stable manager
has agreed to stand in for you. If I remember aright,
Lucy said you had no people of your own.'

He was like some dreadful juggernaut, demolishing
every defence she tried to erect. Jess drew the last frail
arrow in her quiver.

'What about the bridesmaid?' She knew there was only one, who to save time had had her own dress made locally.

'The bridesmaid was Lucy's young cousin. I hardly think, under the circumstances, it would be appropriate for her to come to our wedding, although I'm sure someone else could be persuaded to take her place if you really want an attendant.'

'I don't.'

Her last frail defence crumbled. Jess wanted as few people as possible to witness her humiliation.

'That ties up everything nicely, then, doesn't it?'

Like a parcel, Jess thought raggedly. Tied in a knot. The marriage knot, in five days' time. She felt her senses begin to reel.

'I don't... I can't...' she began wildly. As if in a dream she felt Max lift her nerveless left hand and slide the ruby and diamond ring on to its third finger.

'It fits as if it was made for you,' he observed with satisfaction, and, encircling her slender waist with steel hands, as inexorably as the ring encircled her finger, he bent his dark head above her and silenced her agonised protests with his lips.

CHAPTER TWO

'I'LL marry you. I've got no choice.' Jess wrenched
herself free from Max's arms, and rounded on him furiously. 'But it'll be a marriage in name only. *In name
only,* do you understand?' she flung at him.

The possibility of bearing Max a child haunted her.

He was blackmailing her into this marriage, but while
she remained her own person she could work in secret
to make her name in the fashion world, and then, when
she had become well enough known, and acquired sufficient capital to be able to stand on her own feet and
shrug off any retaliation that Max might attempt, she
would take infinite pleasure in returning his unwanted
wedding ring to him.

Unwittingly, by forcing her to marry him, Max was
opening up to Jess the very social circle into which her
work as a designer needed to penetrate in order to be
able to succeed. The circle which Lucy's elopement had
so very nearly closed to her. Max thought he was re-
venging himself upon her, Jess, for Lucy's defection.
Well, she would secretly take her own revenge upon him,
by using her position as his wife as a stepping-stone in
the very career which he had threatened to wreck, and
when the longed-for day arrived that she could do so
with impunity, she would toss his ring back at him and
leave him flat, Jess vowed.

She could not do that if they had a child.

She would walk out on Max without a backwards
glance. But to leave a child behind—her own flesh and

blood—would be like tearing herself in two. Just the thought of it turned Jess's veins to ice.

There must be no child of this marriage.

Max could not prevent her, Jess, from leaving him when the time was ripe, but she had not the slightest doubt that he would fight for the custody of any child of his. And win.

Who could deny that Blythe Castle could offer a better home to a child that the care that she herself, as a working mother, would be able to provide? If she bore him a child, Max would make her pay the ultimate penalty for her freedom.

He cut through the jumble of her thoughts with a curt, 'We'll discuss that later.'

'Later won't do. We must talk about it now. We must come to an agreement.'

'OK, I agree—for now. So collect your things together.'

He was unstoppable. He took charge with a ruthless energy that swept aside any attempt she tried to make to return to the subject that was uppermost on her mind.

'Sort out the things that belong to you, and I'll order a van to come round and pick them up,' he said, at the same time reaching for the telephone. 'Is that all?' He cast a disparaging look at the open cupboard which contained her sparse wardrobe.

'It's all I need,' Jess snapped.

It was beginning to dawn upon her just what marrying Max Beaumont would mean. So far, Jess had been accustomed to running her own life. In spite of the constraints occasioned by lack of cash, being self-employed gave her a certain freedom of choice, and the curb of the reins as wielded by Max galled her independent spirit.

'What's the hurry? I shan't be leaving here for a day or two,' she rebelled.

'It's the last day of the month today. There's no point in wasting money on a month's advance rent in order to renew a tenancy you won't need after next Wednesday.'

His point was unarguable. Jess bit her lip. Her scarce resources would leave her with very little left over after she had paid for another month's rent.

'Where am I supposed to live in the meantime?'

'At the castle, of course. Throw your clothes into a suitcase.' His tone said it would only need to be a very small one, which was a fair description of her battered holdall anyway, and Jess flushed. 'We'll take them with us in the car, and the van can collect the rest.'

'What about the clothes I made for Lucy?' They draped the picture rail, enclosed in plastic bags, and covered two entire walls of the room, to say nothing of the capacious box filled with handmade lingerie of every colour and description, and the array of casual wear enclosed in a portable wardrobe, in which Jess had invested to keep the short-stay clothes she made for her clients.

'Forget Lucy.' His harsh tone said he was trying to take his own advice, and he bored on impatiently before Jess could answer. 'If you haven't had any money for the clothes, they belong to you, so get them packed.' He intercepted Jess's glance towards the billowing folds of the wedding gown. 'If you're worried about folding that, it can lie across the back seat of the car during the journey home.'

He spoke as if the castle was already home to them both, and interrupted Jess's sharp disclaimer with a decisive, 'You can't possibly be married from here.'

'I suppose you think a bedsitter in a back street isn't good enough for your bride-to-be?' Jess maligned her tiny but convenient accommodation, even while she stubbornly defended it.

Max shot her a steely look. 'Bedsitter or mansion, it's beside the point. It's simply too far away. Unless, of course, you don't mind getting up very early, and driving for several hours in your wedding dress to be at Norton Wood church in time for the ceremony. It's fixed for ten o'clock in the morning.'

He was telling *her*. It should have been the other way round. A choking feeling rose in Jess's throat, stifling her voice, and before she could manage to clear it Max made the decision for her with an authoritative statement to her landlady, who chose that moment to tap on the door and walk in, in the expectation of receiving her customary cheque for the next month's rent.

'My fiancée won't be needing her room after today,' he announced without preliminaries.

Mrs Hodges' bright eyes widened. They darted to where the glittering ring seemed to burn a brand like a manacle into the shrinking flesh of Jess's finger, and returned, blinking, to the aristocratic figure of its donor.

Jess did not doubt that those same eyes had already taken detailed note of the two previous visits from the sleek maroon Jaguar to a kerb that was more accustomed to providing parking space for milk floats and bread vans, and the landlady had probably discussed the stranger endlessly with her cronies in the neighbourhood.

With an obvious effort, Mrs Hodges found the use of her voice, and it rose in an indignant pipe. 'Miss Donaldson didn't give me any notice that she would be leaving. What about my rent?'

'She didn't know herself, until a few minutes ago.'

Max left the landlady to make what she pleased of his cryptic statement, and, taking a leather wallet from out of his top pocket, produced sufficient notes to change the pipe into a satisfied purr.

Adding another note of generous denomination, he instructed, 'Will you please send on any mail you might receive for Miss Donaldson, to this address?' He accompanied a gold-edged visiting card with a pleasant smile.

Her landlady's gurgle of shock as she read the address on the small oblong pasteboard might have amused Jess if she had not been too startled herself by the unexpected sweetness of Max's smile. It was the first one she had seen him give, and it did the most curious things to his face. Almost as curious as the things it was doing to her pulse-rate.

It curved up the corners of his firm, well-cut lips, the slight fullness of the lower one betraying a sensuous depth to his nature that was effectively hidden by his well-controlled exterior. It softened the stern, almost harsh lines of his lean face, and made him look younger, and more handsome, if possible, than before. It ... Jess caught up her wandering thoughts sharply, in time to hear him say, 'Here's the van drawing up now. Are you sure you've got everything?'

The next few minutes were a confusion of Jess's farewells to her landlady, and Max's instructions to the van driver, who unemotionally stowed away all her worldly goods into one corner of his vehicle, to convey them to their new home on which Jess had not yet set eyes herself.

The choking feeling came back with redoubled force, and Jess's eyes were overbright as she returned her landlady's farewell embrace with a fervour which took the redoubtable Mrs Hodges by surprise.

During Jess's tenancy, the two had remained on amicable but rather reserved terms, but suddenly the enormity of what she was about to undertake engulfed Jess, and her landlady represented the mother figure in the only real home she had known since her grandparents had died in New Zealand.

For a second or two she clung to Mrs Hodges' well-corseted frame, and then Max put his arm about her shoulders and drew her firmly away towards the car, with an observation that scarcely registered through the turmoil of Jess's mind. 'The van driver says he can take your wedding dress as well. He's got a hanging rail, and plenty of space.'

Jess did not answer. She felt beyond speech. Mrs Hodges' voice followed her like a mockery as Max guided her towards the car.

'Be happy, dearie.'

Happiness was not in the contract, Jess thought bitterly. In spite of her efforts to subdue it, a low, strangled sound escaped her as the big car took to the motorway. Max glanced across at her from the driving seat, and, without slackening speed he enquired, 'What's the matter?'

'Oh, nothing. Nothing at all. I'm over the moon about the whole wretched business. Surely you can see that?'

'Look on the positive side. After all, you're not getting a bad bargain. As my wife, you'll be Lady Blythe, and mistress of Blythe Castle.'

'Big deal. From where I'm sitting, it's a costly bargain.'

'It's one that not many girls would refuse.'

'Modest, aren't you?' Jess jeered and saw his jaw tighten, but did not care. 'I feel more like a prisoner being dragged off to the castle dungeon.'

'That's an odd way to describe a bride on the way to her wedding.'

'I don't feel like a bride.'

Bride sacrifice would be more to the point. Her own words to Lucy came back to haunt her as the Jaguar steadily ate up the miles, leaving all the hopes and dreams of her old life behind her, and speeding her inexorably towards she knew not what in the new one.

They turned off the motorway and ate a late lunch at a village pub, and somehow Jess managed to force the unwanted food down her throat. She would need all her strength in order to withstand Max.

From then on the journey took them along quieter roads, and soon low border hills began to make restful contours for the eye, folding into green distances that must eventually, Jess surmised, rise into the craggier heights of the Welsh mountains.

Black and white timber-framed farmhouses took the place of the red brick of the Home Counties, each with the tilted roof of an oast-house pointing a conical finger to the sky.

Perforce Max had to reduce speed to accommodate the narrow, winding country roads, and unconsciously the more sedate pace, and the peaceful scenery, induced a measure of calm to ease the turmoil of Jess's mind.

She could not restrain a small gasp of pleasure as a dip in the road revealed a sea of pink orchard blossom spread out below them, and the beauty of it caught at her throat. No matter what she felt about the reason for her journey, this land of low, rolling hills and lush valleys, unaccountably tugged at her heart-strings.

Max glanced across at her, catching the sound, and remarked laconically, 'We're in cider-making country.' And, a few miles further on, 'Hops,' he explained briefly as the car rolled by well-tended acres bristling with long rows of poles, intertwined with a veritable cats' cradle of string, up which climbed young, green plants, reaching eager fingers to the sun.

The road became a lane, which followed a gently flowing river bordering fields dotted with fat lambs, and

Max said, 'That's the Blythe, the river we take our title
from. It runs into the River Wye further along its course.'

We... Jess tensed. Soon, she would be part of that
royal 'we'. Very soon. A signpost pointed the way to
Norton Wood a short half-mile distant, so the castle must
be very close.

When it came in sight she received a shock. The
building stood on rising ground, which was to be
expected, but its size was definitely not expected, and
forced from her a surprised ejaculation. 'It's a lot smaller
than I expected.'

She had not allowed herself to visualise what her new
home would be like, resisting its coming hold upon her
until the last possible moment, but the title of castle
evoked a vision of grandiose, Windsor-like proportions,
with soaring towers, and awe-inspiring battlements, the
vague picture helped not a little by Max's attitude of
arrogant self-confidence that would fit into such a regal
background.

True, the building confronting her possessed battlements, and narrow archery slits in the walls, but the castle
itself was on a comparatively small scale compared to
the imposing monuments she was familiar with in and
around London, and the discovery went a long way
towards reducing the nervousness which Jess had
derided, but which she had been totally unable to control
as they neared their destination.

'Disappointed?' Max sent her a derisive look.

'I'm not interested, either way,' Jess shrugged indif-
ferently. 'I just thought that anything qualifying as a
castle must be...'

'...as big as Windsor? Not the border castles. They're
mostly like Blythe, just fortified manor houses. They
were built like this to withstand sporadic raids caused
by purely local feuds, rather than to repel invading

armies. Blythe has been home to the Beaumonts since the early thirteen hundreds,' he added casually.

Six hundred years of living and loving. Jess's eyes rested bleakly on the ancient stonework. Did ever a more reluctant bride cross its ancient drawbridge?

The bridge was now a fixed, tarmac structure spanning the wide moat, which had been skilfully transformed into a sunken garden, bright now with a colourful spring display.

The colour, however, did nothing to detract from the grim look of the studded oak doors which the car approached at a crawl. Within feet of the barrier, Max leaned forward and touched slim fingers to a button on the car's console, and the doors swung inwards automatically to his unseen signal, betraying smoothly running, modern mechanism behind the ancient exterior. Jess could not repress a shiver as they drove through, and the doors closed again behind them with well-oiled efficiency.

She felt trapped.

She gave a hunted look behind her as Max drove across a courtyard, and her strained eyes met only the unbroken line of impregnable walls and two stout doors through which only those who knew the signal could pass.

It brought home to her, as nothing else could have done, how vulnerable she would be as Max's wife, and she vowed again, with even more fervour than before, I must not have his child.

Another surprise awaited Jess when an approaching archway revealed the house beyond. It bore out Max's description of a manor house, much larger than the farms she had seen during their journey, but reflecting their magpie colouring, and attractively higgledy-piggledy, as if bits had been added to it over the centuries. These had blended together to make a mellow whole, which rested tranquilly among bright gardens. An unexpected pang passed through Jess. If only things had been different, how she would have loved to live in such a place.

Before her startled mind had time to come to grips with its own traitorous thought, the car stopped, and Max was out of his own seat and round the long bonnet, opening the door on her side, and reaching in to help her to alight, and then retrieving her battered suitcase from the boot.

The house door opened as they walked together up the stone steps, and Jess thought disbelievingly, Max must carry a control button in his pocket as well.

The activator proved to be of human origin this time, however. A small, white-haired, birdlike woman, not unlike Jess's ex-landlady, but with a markedly different accent when she spoke, held the door wide and greeted Max. 'The rooms are ready, just as you wanted them, sir.'

Rooms in the plural, Jess noted alertly. At least Max was having the decency to abide by the conventions until they were married.

Afterwards...

'This is Miss Donaldson, Florence. Mrs Kirk, my housekeeper.'

Max cut across Jess's burdened thoughts with an introduction, and she pulled herself together and forced a smile, which was not returned with the woman's coldly formal, 'How do you do, miss?'

Guarded eyes, blank with lack of welcome, summed Jess up, and the housekeeper gave her hand the briefest of grips before letting it go.

Perhaps Mrs Kirk was comparing her to Lucy, and finding her wanting? Jess surmised. Or even wishing that Max had chosen Nina Vaughan instead? What a shock the woman would get if she knew how I wished the same, Jess thought grimly, and gritted her teeth as the house-keeper enquired stiffly, 'Shall I ask the gardener to collect Miss Donaldson's luggage from the car, sir?'

Her disapproving look said the elderly suitcase resting on the floor between them could not possibly be termed luggage, and Jess seethed inwardly as Max saved her from having to reply.

'The luggage is following us on by van. It should be here within the next hour or so. When it arrives, will you have the maid attend to my fiancée's clothes, please, Florence, and make sure the gardener handles the sewing machine with care? It's of sentimental value to Miss Donaldson.'

He met Jess's shocked look with a steely glance that told her he had chosen his words deliberately.

As a warning? Or as a challenge?

Sentimental value. The phrase ping-ponged back-wards and forwards in Jess's heated mind. Max must have divined her intention to carry on working in secret after they were married, and this was his means of telling her that he would make sure she had no opportunity to do anything of the kind, by deliberately relegating her precious sewing machine to the past, as a monument that would have no future place in her life.

We'll see about that, she fumed silently, and her eyes returned his look with the light of battle in them.

With the merest suggestion of a shrug to his broad shoulders, he turned away with the housekeeper to ascend the graceful, winding staircase, and with an immense effort Jess choked back the angry words that sprang to her lips, and thought incredulously as she followed the two upwards, I haven't been here for many minutes, and I'm already learning the ropes. Conforming to the un-written, 'not in front of the servants' rule, that de-

manded she keep her thoughts to herself until she and
Max were alone. By that time the opportunity would be
past, and the impact would be lost, overlaid by half a
dozen other happenings that would defuse the anger, and
make the words which burned her tongue now not worth
the speaking.

What a perfect recipe for a happy marriage, she
thought bleakly. It was a built-in cooling-off time for all
sorts of domestic tiffs.

When she left Max, there would be no argument. By
then she too would be in a position of strength, unas-
sailable, and she would choose her time to go when Max
was not around, and so could not take measures to
prevent her.

The present had to be lived through before that day
came, however, and the housekeeper was asking, 'Would
you like something to eat now, sir, or would you prefer
to wait until later?'

Mrs Kirk spoke to Max directly, Jess noticed, and not
to both of them, silently emphasising that, until they
were married, Jess must regard herself as being a guest
at the castle, and not its mistress. In fact, that she, Mrs
Kirk, was still in charge.

Jess burned at the calculated relegation, and felt a
small triumph when Max redeemed it somewhat by unexpectedly deferring to her choice.

'Not unless Jess feels hungry? We ate on the way
down.' He looked askance. Jess shook her head, and he
decided, 'We'll wait for dinner. I want to see Bob about
the stallion as soon as I've changed. Will you come with
me, Jess, or would you prefer to rest after the journey?'

Jess scorned his solicitude, which she was sure was
only play-acting for the benefit of his housekeeper. She
would have preferred to remain in her room, but, 'I'll
come with you,' she answered reluctantly.

Better the devil she knew, than to remain under the basilisk scrutiny of Mrs Kirk. She could rest later. Indeed, it would be the perfect excuse for her to retire early, after dinner was over, and thus save herself the strain of an unwanted evening in Max's company.

'I'll meet you downstairs in fifteen minutes, then.'

He dropped her suitcase in a nearby room and strode away along the landing, leaving Mrs Kirk to follow Jess inside.

'I hope you'll be comfortable in here until Wednesday night, Miss Donaldson,' the latter said significantly, and Jess felt her cheeks begin to burn, made hotter still by the knowledge that the sharp eyes of the other woman missed nothing of the confusion she had caused.

Until Wednesday night. Jess felt her hands turn clammy.

The room she entered was charmingly furnished along simple lines designed to make a guest as comfortable as possible for the period of a short stay.

She would occupy it for only a few nights, and then...

What then? Jess scorned to ask the housekeeper what arrangements Max had ordered. No doubt it would give Mrs Kirk considerable satisfaction if she did so, but, tight-lipped, Jess resisted the temptation. She longed to know, if only to spare herself the ordeal of broaching the subject with Max again. Max had agreed to a marriage in name only 'for now'. Had he any intention of keeping his promise? And how long would his 'for now' last?

He was devastatingly attractive, and well aware of the fact. Young, virile, in the first full strength of his manhood, his position ensured that he was accustomed to getting his own way.

Jess did not make the mistake of underestimating the power of her own winsome beauty, either. Although her lovely bone structure and delicate features might not compare with Lucy's immature prettiness in Max's eyes, she was here and Lucy was not, and the combination threatened a heady brew that might ferment, and eventually erupt if she was not very careful. If that happened, the results might well be catastrophic, not only for her immediate plans, but for her future happiness as well.

Conscious that her hands were clenching into two tight fists of tension, Jess thrust them deep into the pockets of her coat, and became aware that Mrs Kirk was still awaiting her answer.

'Most comfortable, thank you,' she managed. 'The room is quite charming.'

She dragged her mind back to immediate matters, and tried to close it to the future alternative as Mrs Kirk spoke again.

'Will you change before you go downstairs again, miss? Shall I empty your suitcase for you?'

'There's nothing in it that I need, thank you. I'll go downstairs as I am. All my clothes are following in a van.'

Jess felt thankful that her shabby holdall was locked, and she resisted the housekeeper's silent assumption that she should be given the key in order to unpack it.

Her clothes were of good quality. She had designed and made them herself. But, because they were few in quantity, they were all well worn, not to say shabby, and she had no intention of allowing them to be subjected to the inquisitive eyes of a stranger.

'The van should have arrived by the time Max and I get back,' she said firmly. 'I'll change then.'

She no longer felt any qualms about appropriating the clothes she had made for Lucy. Her erstwhile client no longer needed them, and since she had paid for all

the materials, to say nothing of the work that had gone
into making them up, she could rightfully claim them
as her possessions.

She knew the outfit she was wearing at the moment
was beyond reproach. She had designed and made it for
her final exams at college, and it had, she felt con-
vinced, been largely responsible for the coveted honours
level of her final passing-out results.

The beech-brown wool skirt fitted her slender figure
like a glove, topped by a hand-embroidered cream silk
blouse with rich lace inserts at collar and cuffs, and a
brown and cream dog's-tooth check coat with a loose
swing back, and edged with the same material as her
skirt.

She could claim that the outfit was a model in every
sense of the word, which should satisfy even Mrs Kirk's
obviously exacting standards. Jess felt grateful to
whatever instinct had made her resist the many requests
she had received after the end of term show was over to
sell the outfit to envious friends, and reap immediate
benefit from the much-needed cash it would have
brought her.

She looked good, and knew it, and the confidence it
brought her helped her to dismiss the housekeeper with
a cool, 'I won't keep you from your duties any longer.
Just put the case into the wardrobe, while I freshen up.
I don't want to keep Max waiting. He's anxious for news
of the stallion.'

She knew nothing about the stallion, but her companion was not to know that, and if she was to be forced
into filling the position of mistress of Blythe Castle, for
however brief a time, she did not intend to spend that
time in a role subservient to the housekeeper.

Mrs Kirk would no doubt enjoy considerable powers
in a bachelor household, and Jess sensed that if she did

not assert herself now her position at the castle would be even more impossible than it promised to be already.

The older woman hesitated for what seemed a long moment, but Jess kept her gaze steady, and at last, with compressed lips, the housekeeper bent and picked up the suitcase. Jess turned away and shrugged out of her coat, then hid a grin in a soapy lather at the washbasin as the wardrobe door shut none too gently behind her, and soon afterwards the bedroom door followed suit.

Round one to me, she decided with satisfaction, and joined Max downstairs a few minutes later in a more confident frame of mind.

He turned and looked up as she rounded the bend of the staircase, and for a moment her step faltered. Casual clothes did nothing to detract from his astonishing good looks; the black silk, roll-necked sweater and black stretch jeans closely moulded his athletic frame, setting off to advantage lean thighs and broad shoulders, and arms of sinewy strength where he had pushed up his sweater sleeves to give himself added freedom.

As he had so conceitedly asserted, becoming his wife was a position that not many girls would refuse, for the sake of the man as well as for his wealth and title. The fact that she was not among their number did not prevent Jess's very feminine heart from beating a little faster, however, as she forced her feet to continue their descent.

A black and tan setter rose lazily to its feet as she gained the last stair, and Max clicked his fingers and ordered, 'Come and make friends, Shandy.'

'His name fits his colouring.' Jess smiled and held out both her hands to the dog, and did not notice the lingering glance which the man sent in her direction as the setter came forward obediently to nuzzle her fingers.

She liked dogs, and she was more than willing to make friends with this one. She felt as if she needed a friend in this antagonistic household.

'What's the matter with the stallion?' she asked as they moved out of doors together, before Max could speak.

She felt nervous of conversation with this man, who in a few short days would be her husband, and whom she scarcely knew. During their journey to the castle it had been comparatively easy to remain silent and watch the passing scenery, while Max concentrated on driving, but they could not remain together for ever without speaking, and suddenly Jess shrank from the possibility that he might broach a more intimate topic, however much she needed an answer to the question that troubled her.

This would have to be faced later, but not yet. Not today. She still had a few days of grace until the wedding.

'There's nothing the matter with him. Quite the reverse, in fact. He had his first big race today, and I want to know how he got on.'

'Race?' Her look was an open question, inviting him to expand on a topic that was safe.

'Harness racing,' Max obliged. 'You'll see, when we get to the paddocks.'

'If you were so keen to know how the stallion got on, why didn't you go along and see for yourself?'

'Bob went instead. I had more important things to do.'

'Like hijacking a bride?'

Max muttered something low and fierce under his breath as he turned on her, and Jess's eyes widened at the fury in his. His face darkened with anger, and he ground out, 'Say that again, and I'll...'

What he would do was lost in the sudden clatter of a lawn-mower. A gnarled figure appeared round the corner of a shrubbery and steered the machine in their direction, further barbering what Jess had considered to be an already immaculate greensward.

Max broke off, and responded with a courteous word as the gardener greeted them with, 'Afternoon, sir, miss. Lovely day.' And passed on, taking his noise with him.

'We'll use the Range Rover to go down to the paddocks,' Max said abruptly when the clatter faded into the distance, and he swung off along a path towards a stable block that was evidently used as a garage, and was hidden from the house by the shrubbery.

'I'm used to walking.'

Jess did not add that walking had up to now been an economic necessity, but Max replied, 'Another time, when you're wearing flat-heeled shoes.'

He did not refer again to his threat, nor to her taunt which drew it, and Jess thought, the cooling off period works both ways, as he helped her up into the high seat beside him.

The encircling castle walls were crumbled to merely a low barrier on this side of the building, opening out a wide view of parkland and hills, and allowing the gardens to run right down to the edge of the river, from where a wide stone bridge gave free access to the rising fields beyond.

Jess drew in a long breath, and as she let it out again the awful sense of claustrophobia which had gripped her since they came through the doors of the drawbridge went with it.

She would, after all, be free to come and go as she pleased from the castle, without being obliged to ask Max each time to unlock the entrance doors for her.

When the time came for her to leave him, the way would be wide open.

Max scanned the terrain in front of them with narrowed eyes, and discovered, 'There's Bob Tempest, in the lower paddock.' He pointed to the distant figure of a man sitting astride a high wooden fence, which Jess saw enclosed a spacious paddock housing a single horse.

Max turned the Range Rover in that direction, and their present elevation allowed Jess a clear view as they drove beside numerous other paddocks, each bordered by the same well-kept paling fences, and holding horses in varying numbers.

Further on rose the low profile of stables and barns, and what appeared to be the fenced off oval shape of a purpose-built track.

'A race-track?' she exclaimed. 'You go in for your hobbies in a big way, don't you?' The contrast between their situations stung, and this further evidence of his affluence laced her voice with unconscious bitterness as she taunted, 'Nice to inherit the sort of money that allows you to indulge.'

Max's eyes glinted, and he shot back, 'All that I inherited was a title, and an estate saddled with a load of death duties. I had to start from scratch the same as you, in order to pull the place together again.'

That his pulling had been a superlative success was abundantly clear by the condition of the property she had seen so far, and Jess's silence accorded his efforts the same grudging respect that he had earlier shown for her own as he went on, 'Harness racing is big business overseas, and growing fast in this country. I would have thought you'd know that, coming from New Zealand. It's a popular sport down under.'

'I never went to the race-tracks at home. We lived too far away from them, although I've seen the racing on television, of course.'

Jess knew it to be a lucrative occupation for those who were lucky enough to be at the top, and her surroundings here bore this out. There was an air of caring prosperity about the estate which she had already seen reflected in the excellent state of preservation of the castle itself.

Had Liz really meant it, she wondered, when she'd described Max as a millionaire with a title? At the time, Jess had dismissed the remark as mere off-the-cuff teasing, but belatedly she remembered that Liz had mentioned going to harness-racing meetings herself since she had married. Her husband was a fan of the sport, and through him Liz might be familiar with Max's name in connection with the race-tracks.

Jess frowned. So many questions. So few satisfactory answers. Max asked a question of his own.

'Were you interested enough to follow the sport?'

'I wasn't, then.'

'Are you now?'

Jess did not know how to answer him.

She was not interested in Max, nor his title, nor his millions if he had them. She lumped them all together and loathed the whole package. But she could not help being interested in the horses.

She had learned to ride as a child in New Zealand, but the opportunity to take up the hobby seriously had not come her way, and the borrowed mounts that had carried her then could by no stretch of imagination boast any particular ancestry.

The horses in these paddocks were superb. One and all, they carried the majestic lines of impeccable breeding. Proud heads lifted to watch the Range Rover pass, before lowering again to the lush grass on which they grazed.

Even the spindly-legged foals that gambolled awkwardly around their dams bore the same thoroughbred stamp, and Jess yearned to leave the vehicle to have a closer look at them. She was enchanted by the foals, and unable to hide it, so she used her delight in their antics as a subterfuge to avoid having to reply to Max's unanswerable question.

'I love horses,' she prevaricated.

'Do you ride?'

'I used to, a little, before I started college.'

After that, she had lost the only family she had ever known, and gained a scholarship to study in England, since when there had been neither the time nor the money to enable her to indulge her pleasure.

She was saved from enlarging as the Range Rover approached the side of the paddock where the man sat astride the fence, talking quietly to a tall, fiery-looking grey on the other side, tossing its head.

'Is that the stallion?' Jess asked interestedly.

'Yes, that's Cloud,' answered Max. 'Keep your fingers crossed that he acquitted himself well on the track.'

'Why, did you have a bet on him winning?'

Max threw her an oblique look. 'There's a lot more at stake here than just money.'

He spoke as if money did not matter, and perhaps to him it didn't. Jess's lips twisted. He might not be overly interested in his wealth, but he had no scruples in using it as a weapon to force other people to do what he wanted.

He went on, 'Cloud's the first to mature in a new strain I'm breeding. It's a long-term thing. He's four years old now, and beginning to work well in harness, but my hunch in choosing his sire and dam will stand or fall by his performance. As will his own use at stud later on, of course. You have to choose the pedigree carefully to bring out the points you need in a foal. There's no room for mistakes.'

Jess turned her head and studied the strong, proud face beside her. Max's pride was at stake, and that, to him, would be more important than all the gold of the Incas. She retorted bitterly, 'You're more careful about the pedigree of your horses than you are of your wife. For all you know, you could be making a ghastly mistake in marrying me. You know nothing about me. Why don't you marry Nina Vaughan instead? Lucy told me she'd be more than willing, and at least you know her background. You don't know mine.'

'I choose my own wife.'

'Why choose me?'

There was still time to back out, Jess hoped desperately, but Max destroyed her wishful thinking with a dry, 'Let's say your conformation looked right.'

Jess's anger erupted. 'I'm not one of your horses. And I'm certainly not a thoroughbred.'

She talked to deaf ears. Max leaned through the window and called out to the man, who quit his seat astride the fence and strolled to meet them as the Range Rover rolled to a stop.

'How did Cloud get on, Bob?'

The stallion was of more importance to Max than his future wife. Anger surged inside Jess, and bitter resentment, but there was no time to vent her feelings, because the middle-aged man was already at the vehicle door, and in a voice that held a hint of soft Kerry burr he replied, 'Cloud did fine. He came second. He could have made a sprint at the end, but I didn't let him overstretch himself. He was running well within his stride, and I couldn't fault his performance. You can decide when to let him out when you're racing him yourself.'

There was the hint of a question in his voice, and in the look he cast at Jess, but all Max said was, 'I'll do that. We'll come and have a look at him now.' He sniffed the air, and said apropos of nothing, 'Are you wearing perfume, Jess?'

'No.' She shook her head. That was another luxury she was unable to afford. She enjoyed wearing good perfume, and would rather do without it than use cheap brands. She looked her puzzlement. 'Why?'

Max's tone was dry. 'Because the musk in perfume has the same effect on an excitable young stallion as the adverts would like women to believe it has on the human male.'

His eyes derided her rising colour, while his next words held a serious warning. 'Thoroughbreds are highly strung, and the stallions can be dangerous. I'll get you some perfume made from pure flower oils that will be safe for you to wear when you're around the stables.'

Jess did not intend to be around at all for any longer than she could help, but she let it pass, and responded to Bob Tempest's handshake with a smile that was unforced.

She liked the stocky Irishman on sight, and his cheerful addition to Max's introduction of him as, 'Trainer and stable manager,' drew a chuckle from her that brought Max's eyes swiftly round to rest on her animated face.

'Groom, midwife, nurse, and general factotum as well,' Bob included ruefully, and offered, 'You must have a mount for yourself.'

'It will have to be a quiet one,' Jess responded promptly. 'I haven't been on a horse for years.'

'I'll set aside a couple of mares for your use,' Max said, but he did not say when, and, although Jess was

determined to escape from what she could only regard
as her bondage, cutting those bonds would take time,
and she hoped he would not forget his promise. Riding
would serve as the perfect antidote when the tension between them got more than she could bear, and she might
as well gain something from their forced marriage.

If all the animals in the castle stables were of the same
calibre as those she had seen in the paddocks, her
pleasure would be assured, and probably never repeated
after she left Max, she acknowledged.

She owned no formal riding kit, but that did not
matter. Denims and trainers had served her well enough
before, and would have to do so now.

She leaned over the fence between the two men and
watched as Max reached into his pocket and drew out
an apple, and split it into sections with the aid of his
strong, supple fingers that did not need to recourse to
a knife for the purpose.

He took the sections piece by piece and offered them
flat-palmed to the stallion, which tossed its head and at
first pretended indifference, but bit by bit minced slowly
forward, and accepted them delicately from the man's
hand.

Max raised his head, and his grey eyes, that could be
so cold, warmed to the majestic creature that came to
his bidding. Jess thought, startled, that the same description could apply to them both.

Both were magnificent specimens of their own kind,
each accepting allegiance on the other's terms, and,
watching the picture they made together, Jess felt an unexpected pang that could have been pleasure, or could
have been pain, and was probably a mixture of both.

The last quarter of the apple eaten, Max turned away
from the rail and said, 'You must learn to drive a sulky
as well, Jess. Bob will teach you to start with. I shan't

have much time myself until after the County Show is over.'

You *must* learn to drive. Not, would you like to?

Resentment at his dictatorial attitude destroyed the handsome picture in Jess's mind. How arrogant he was. How supremely sure of himself. For the duration of their marriage, she determined that Max should accept her on her own terms as well. If, by his offer of perfume and such like gifts, he imagined she would be prepared to come meekly to his hand like the stallion, he had yet to discover his mistake.

Bob Tempest took up the conversation. 'Speaking of the County Show, Max, your name's the one on the racecard, as driver, and I think it's too late to alter it now. Will you cancel? I mean...' He broke off, and his gaze swivelled a silent question at Jess.

'If you mean, will we be away on our honeymoon, the answer's no,' Max retorted. 'We've decided to postpone it until after the show is over. As the castle is hosting it this year, I can't possibly delegate, and since I've got to be here anyway, I might as well drive in the race.'

Indirectly, Max was telling her that there was to be no honeymoon. Relief, anger, and an aching kind of pain, warred inside Jess at the news. It should not be like this. *They* had not decided. Max had decided and, so far as he was concerned, that was that.

He was forcing her to go through with this marriage, and all the while he was taking a sadistic pleasure in taunting her with its hollow mockery, emphasising his power over her.

Jess hated him with a fierce hatred for what he was doing to her, so intense that it trampled into silence the desolation inside her, which mourned again.

If only things had been different.

CHAPTER THREE

MAX did all the expected things calculated to paint the conventional picture of a happy, betrothed couple, Jess thought scornfully.

He showed her with unconcealed pride round the immaculate stables, humoured her plea to be allowed to have a closer look at the foals, had a sulky harnessed and drove it round the oval track himself at a racing trot, so that she should have a close look at the action of the horse, and the skeleton carriage which it pulled. The carriage was little more, she saw interestedly, than a pair of wheels and shafts, and a spartan seat just wide enough to carry the driver.

Jess stood beside Bob and watched Max's expert handling of the frail-seeming buggy, and she could not help but thrill to the possibility of driving one herself, even as she wondered how much the stable manager knew about the real reason for her being here.

What explanation, if any, had Max put abroad for his sudden change of bride? None, she guessed accurately. Max was not a man to bare his heart in confidences to anyone. If, indeed, he had a heart at all, hidden away behind the self-sufficient exterior that the world saw as Lord Blythe.

After one circuit of the track, a stable lad took over the horse and sulky, and led them away, and Max said, 'We're pushing dinner time. We'd better go back now. See you later, Bob.'

He talked horses on the short drive back, and Jess was content to follow his lead. It eased the atmosphere between them slightly, and when she wondered out loud if her clothes had arrived, he retorted confidently, 'Of course they'll have come. They were due an hour ago.' As if anything which he had arranged could possibly go wrong!

Jess bit back a sharp reply. Suddenly the traumas of the day caught up with her, and she felt too weary to want to fight Max any more tonight. Almost, she wished her clothes had not arrived, and she could use their lack as an excuse to remain in her room.

The prospect of eating under the critical eye of Florence Kirk took away her appetite, but when she regained her room she found the new clothes neatly hung and folded in the ample space provided for them. Her sewing machine, too, had been carefully placed in a corner of her bedroom. A quick check reassured her that it had survived the journey unscathed.

A lump choked Jess's throat as she ran her hand over the polished case. The machine was her sole link with her freedom, and her only means of regaining it.

She donned her own favourite among several evening dresses that she had made for Lucy. It was a floor-length, leaf-green sheath that made a perfect foil for her chestnut hair, and for the subtle undertones that lightened or darkened her clear hazel eyes according to her mood.

They darkened when Mrs Kirk announced her intention to send up a maid to help her to dress, and Jess resisted the intrusion with a firm, 'I prefer to manage on my own, thank you.'

Which sent that worthy away with the uneasy conviction that this outsider, whom nobody knew anything at all about, and who Mr Max had suddenly produced in Miss Lucy's place with never a word of explanation to anyone—she had checked with Bob Tempest to make sure, and the stable manager told her that it had come

as just as big a surprise to him as well—this new broom
had got some unexpectedly stiff bristles, which showed
signs of sweeping into all sorts of corners they had no
need to.

If it had been Miss Lucy, now, or even that Miss
Vaughan who kept hanging round the master...either
would have been only too willing to leave things to go
on just as they always had done, with never a thought
to go against anything that she, Florence Kirk, suggested.

This Miss Donaldson was a different kettle of fish
altogether. She had a mind of her own and used it, and
to make matters worse she spoke with the trace of an
accent which Mrs Kirk could not place, as if she might
be a foreigner.

The housekeeper tut-tutted her way back to the
kitchen. What with one bride gone and another taking
her place, entirely out of the blue, she didn't know
whether she was on her head or her heels, she com-
plained to Cook.

Mrs Kirk felt aggrieved, and showed it, and Jess could
not help feeling relieved when a maid appeared to serve
them at dinner instead of the older woman.

She felt even more relieved when Bob Tempest joined
them in the drawing-room after the meal was over, effectively putting off the time when she and Max must
be alone together.

'Horses again,' the stable manager apologized. 'I'm
sorry to barge in on you on your first night here, Miss
Donaldson.'

'Since you call Max by his first name, you must call
me Jess.'

'It's quicker, if you don't mind.' The Irishman looked
pleased by the concession, nevertheless, and Jess did not
care what Max thought. His expression gave nothing
away, and he appeared to be intent only on what his

stable manager was saying, as the latter went on, 'I must get Max's OK to one or two things, and the closer we get to Wednesday, the harder it will be to pin him down, I expect. The most important is a farm sale coming up, with a sulky that might prove interesting.'

'Where's the sale being held?' Max enquired.

'In the north, close to York,' replied Bob. 'I've heard on the grapevine that an old sulky has been parked in one of the barns there for some time. The owner of the place was apparently a bachelor, and his only surviving relative lives abroad, and he wants to get rid of the farm and the contents with the least possible trouble to himself. It might be worth going up to see if the sulky can be restored to a workable condition. The only snag is, the sale's next Friday.'

Two days after their wedding.

Max said promptly, 'We'll go. Make sure the Range Rover's ready for the road, will you, Bob?'

'I thought you might prefer to drive the Jag, as Jess will be with you.'

Jess looked up, startled. Somehow she had envisaged the 'we' to include Bob, and not herself. It was difficult to come to terms with the fact that, by Friday, she would be Max's wife, and everyone would take it for granted she would be the one to go along with him.

By then the nightmare would be a reality, and there was absolutely no way in which she could prevent it from happening.

'There might be other things in the sale we want to bring back with us,' Max replied, and Jess felt the choking sense of claustrophobia descend upon her again.

Max did not intend to spare her any of the duties as his wife. She used the stable manager's reiterated apology for interrupting their evening together as an excuse to escape the room, the walls of which suddenly seemed to close in on her like a prison cell, with Max as her gaoler.

'Don't apologise, Bob. I'll leave you two to talk business in peace. It's been a long day, and I'm absolutely dropping.'

'Forgive me. I shouldn't have dragged you round the stables.' Max rose to his feet immediately as Jess stood up and put her empty coffee-cup on to the tray. 'I promise we'll have a more restful day tomorrow. There are only the Vaughans coming to lunch.'

Jess's barbed look said she had a lot more to forgive him than a tour round his stables, and the presence of the Vaughans on the morrow would probably make the day the reverse of restful for her. If Lucy's description of the family was accurate, she would be faced with frustrated, social-climbing parents, and a disappointed contender for the hand of her own unwanted fiancé. What a lunch party! Jess sighed wearily. For her, tomorrow would dawn like a call to arms.

Max's arms. They reached out and captured her, and drew her close against him, and she was too surprised to resist as he murmured solicitously, 'Go up early and get a good night's sleep.'

His lips descended in what the interestedly watching Bob must regard as a loving, lingering kiss. It was the third time Max had kissed her, and its effect lost nothing by repetition. It seared her mouth, branding his claim upon her quivering lips, and Jess went rigid in his close embrace. He moulded her to him, a terrifying reminder of her worst fears, made no easier by the curious, flaring light in the grey eyes looking down at her which warned her that, in spite of being jilted by Lucy, he was not averse to enjoying the experience of kissing another woman.

He held her so close that she knew he must feel the anger and resentment that coursed through her at his touch, but his arms were like steel bands round her, forcing her into compliance, and she knew that her strength was no match in a physical struggle against him.

Not so her will. Fury, resentment and a helpless despair warred in a fiery brew inside her, spiced with an inexplicable mixture of fear and excitement, and something else which she could not define, but which made the cauldron finally boil over.

She wanted to scream at him, I won't marry you. Why should I? You can have your ring back, and do your worst.

She tried to tug at her ring, but his hand moved swiftly to crush hers into stillness. Her tongue got as far as the first, 'I won't...' but stalled as Max's mouth came down again and smothered her own, bruising her lips back against her teeth with a relentless pressure, and stifling the rest of her words before they could form a coherent protest.

Her senses were beginning to swim when he finally let her go. He turned her in the circle of his arm and guided her towards the door; Jess trembled so violently that she had to lean against him for support as she crossed the carpet beside him on uncertain feet.

From behind, they must look like the perfect courting couple, Jess thought raggedly.

She scarcely heard Bob's kindly, 'Goodnight, Jess. Sleep tight.' Her ashen lips were incapable of forming a reply, but the Irishman's smile said he did not seriously expect an answer from a girl who had just been thoroughly kissed by the man she loved.

Max opened the door and paused, and bent his head over her again, brushing his lips tantalisingly across her forehead. His eyes mocked her as she flinched away, and his murmured, 'Goodnight, Jess,' echoed tauntingly through the closing door as he turned back into the room and shut it between them.

Jess's heart hammered. For long seconds she leaned weakly back against the solid wood of the doorpost, fighting faintness, but soon noises from the region of the green baize door which separated the kitchen quarters from the rest of the house warned her that it would be unwise to remain where she was for much longer, if she did not want the interested eyes of the servants to witness her distressed state.

With an immense effort she rallied her swimming senses, and forced herself away from the doorpost to gain the stairs. By dint of using all the strength she had left in her arms, she managed to pull herself step by difficult step up to the landing, and regain the sanctuary of her room.

It would not remain her sanctuary for long.

She undressed with fumbling fingers, and slipped over her head the silk nightdress that she had hand sewn with such pleasure only a few short weeks ago, as part of another girl's trousseau.

Now, it was her own. Reality chased away the enchantment and reaction set in; and Jess flung herself across the bed and allowed the pillow to receive the storm of tears that brought her neither consolation nor relief.

She awoke the next morning with a throbbing headache. Groaning, she swung her legs out of bed and stumbled to the en suite bathroom, and was ducking her face under the cold water tap in an attempt to ease the pain, when someone tapped on the bedroom door.

Max?

Jess's nerves twanged like fiddle strings, and she grabbed for a towel with one hand, and her wrap with the other.

She could not pretend to be still asleep, because whoever stood on the other side of the door must have heard the taps running, and reluctantly she forced herself to call, 'Come in.'

A maid appeared. She released a covered silver tray on to the bedside-table, and said, smiling, 'Mr Max asked me to remind you that the morning service is at ten o'clock at Norton Wood church, Miss Donaldson, not eleven o'clock.'

'Of course.' Jess dredged up an answering smile. 'I'd forgotten.'

She had not known the time in the first place. Max didn't miss a trick, she thought bitterly. He had chosen this way to inform her that he would be attending the morning service himself, and expected her to put in an appearance with him.

Setting a good example to the staff, she thought cynically, and thrust down a wild desire to laugh, and an equally urgent desire to weep.

She had not realised before how precious were those peaceful Sunday mornings spent in the shabby mission hall of a back London street, with its hard wooden benches, and oh, so friendly people, uplifted by the ancient wisdom intoned by an elderly cleric, whom she would never hear preach again.

Did Max guess at the sudden, sickening dread which grabbed her at the prospect of facing the castle staff and villagers, all of whom would know everybody else, except herself, and would be abuzz with curiosity as to why she, and not Lucy, was appearing at Max's side wearing his ring?

Perhaps Max did guess. At all events, he tucked Jess's hand securely through his arm when she presented herself downstairs, having forced down the dainty breakfast set out on the silver tray.

The warm food and drink eased the pain of the headache, but the bruises still remained under Jess's eyes, and she was aware of Max's keen glance raking her face as he asked her unexpectedly, 'Are you wearing comfortable shoes?'

'They're as comfortable as slippers. Why?'

They were dainty, lightweight flatties, and they teamed admirably with the fine wool dress and coat she had donned, guessing from the glimpse she had had of the ancient building as they passed through the village yesterday that the interior of the church might be chilly.

'We all walk to church if it's fine. It's a pleasant stroll, and it isn't far across the park, but it might be difficult walking if you were wearing something for looks instead of comfort.'

The walk turned out to be more like a club ramble, Jess thought, startled. The entire staff of the castle must have turned out, along with their families.

So far, she had met only one or two. She had realised from the perfectly maintained appearance of the place that there must be more but, even so, the numbers surprised her. Max must enjoy an extremely good income to be able to support such a large payroll, which confirmed Liz's description of him, and added to Jess's unease.

Wealth was power. Great wealth meant greater power, and she, Jess, was fighting it unaided. Unconsciously she squared her shoulders and forced her voice to a lightness she did not feel as she exclaimed, 'With all these people, the church will be packed,' gesturing towards the various groups who strolled in scattered bunches to the back and front of them.

'I expect it will be . . . today,' Max replied, with an odd emphasis that raised Jess's eyes in question to his face.

'Isn't it always like this? What's the attraction today?'

'You.'

His sardonic look watched the hot colour rise in Jess's cheeks, but before she could reply they caught up with a strolling group just in front of them, and perforce she had to respond to their pleasantries, all the time aware of their covert scrutiny, particularly from the women.

It was taken up by the village people who were already seated when they got to the church, and Jess knew a moment of panic as they entered the lovely old building, but Max tucked her arm even more firmly through his own and pulled her along with him, as he replied to greetings from right and left on their way along the aisle, to where the castle pew lay at the front.

On Wednesday, she would walk on his arm in the opposite direction, as his wife.

The hour that followed was an ordeal of eyes for Jess. They pinpointed her like a fly on a wall, and she squirmed under the unrelenting surveillance. Nerves sharpened her voice when, at the end of the service, the vicar shook her warmly by the hand, and suggested that she and Max return the following day for a rehearsal of the wedding ceremony.

'No!'

The monosyllable exploded through Jess's set teeth like a bullet from a gun. One wedding ceremony, with Max as her bridegroom, was already too much. Two would be unendurable.

'We'll rely on everything going off all right on the day,' Max intervened, and added urbanely, 'My fiancée's suffering from an attack of pre-wedding nerves.'

Her own diagnosis to Lucy of the same dreadful malady, but without Lucy's remedy. Jess nerved herself to face the coming ordeal of lunch, but she knew the moment the Vaughan family arrived at the castle that the next few hours were going to prove even more difficult than she had anticipated.

The visitors walked straight in as if they owned the castle, and, irritated, Jess vowed silently, *after Wednesday they'll have to ring the bell, the same as everybody else.* She shook hands, knowing that the gesture had been made deliberately to emphasise the Vaughans' prior right under their host's roof, and put Jess out of countenance.

William Vaughan proved to be sleek and shiny, the epitome of the successful city man. He had shrewd, calculating eyes that seemed to be assessing everything they rested upon in terms of Stock Exchange values, and Jess disliked him on sight.

Her antipathy extended to his wife and daughter. Kate Vaughan appeared to be much the same age as her husband. Her unnatural slimness Jess put down to rigid dieting, and the angular result offended her aesthetic sense. Kate's carefully touched-up hair was dressed high, in a style that signally failed in its intention to give the wearer a classic appearance, but was probably the nearest thing to a coronet which she would ever wear.

Jess might have felt pity for the older woman if she had not met the hardness of the pale eyes that told her their owner had not, even at this eleventh hour, abandoned her ambition to see her daughter, and not Jess, wearing Max's ring.

The temptation to snatch off the jewel and present it to Nina, and tell her, *you're welcome,* was almost irresistible, but something held Jess back and the impulse passed. She dragged her attention back to Kate Vaughan, who was saying in an exaggeratedly refined voice, 'Of course, we're used to Max doing the unexpected, but *this . . .*'

She eyed Jess up and down, and her look was a calculated insult. Jess's irritation rose by several notches.

'I assume by this, you mean me?' she enquired sweetly, and saw the pale eyes blink, and knew with satisfaction that her return shot had gone home.

Anger burned inside her. Max's treatment of her was bad enough, but if he assumed that she would put up with similar from others of his circle, he was greatly mistaken.

If she had lacked courage, she would not have crossed the world alone to further her education, and if it came to a battle these people would discover that the spirit of her pioneering ancestors was still very much alive inside her, and a force to be reckoned with.

The second skirmish came as they all adjourned to the dining-room in obedience to the gong.

Max held out the chair on his right hand for Kate Vaughan, and her husband took the one on his other side. The housekeeper, who had elected to serve at table herself this morning, presumably in deference to the supposed importance of the guests, held out the chair opposite to Max, and smiled across at Nina.

Whether it was a genuine mistake on the part of Mrs Kirk, or a deliberate throwing down of the gauntlet between them, Jess did not stop to consider. The chair facing Max was her own, by right of her future position in this household, and no matter what her own feelings about that position might be she had no intention of allowing anyone to usurp it.

With an adroit move she slipped into the chair with a smooth, 'Thank you, Mrs Kirk,' which left the housekeeper with a blank look on her face, and Nina with no option but to take the other, side-of-the-table chair.

She did so with an ill grace, and a look at Jess that warned her she had made an enemy of the other girl.

Not that it made much difference. Nina would regard any girl wearing Max's ring as her enemy.

Youth gave Nina a transitory prettiness, aided by blonde curly hair and blue eyes, but her thin lips betrayed a shrewish nature with would probably manifest itself in spite, Jess surmised.

She turned her attention to something which William Vaughan was saying, and caught the end of his sentence, '...if Cloud can win the cup at the County Show.'

'It isn't always the one who wins the prize who manages to keep it,' Nina butted in waspishly from the other side of the table. Jess thought incredulously, she means me. And Max. Even after we're married, she still intends to carry on fighting for him. The girl's got absolutely no scruples.

She glanced along the table towards Max, but his face remained impassive. Had he taken Nina's remark purely on its face value, as relating to nothing more than harness racing? Was she herself reading more into the other girl's words than was intended?

One look at the brazen challenge in Nina's stare told Jess that she was not mistaken. The knives were out with a vengeance, and not merely as tools to cut the food.

The contretemps with Nina set the pattern for the rest of the lunch party. Jess's nerves were stretched to breaking-point as she parried the loaded comments and barbed remarks from the two Vaughan women, the more obvious of them carefully made out of Max's hearing, until in desperation she exchanged defence for attack. Her change of tactics took the two by surprise, and made them more wary in their approach, but it did nothing to dispel the charged atmosphere between them.

It was almost worse than being alone with Max, Jess thought exhaustedly, then rapidly revised her opinion when, together, they eventually waved the family goodbye from the entrance steps, and turned to go back indoors. Max rounded on her furiously.

'Did you have to be so infernally rude to Kate Vaughan and Nina? Need I remind you that they were guests in my home?'

'They started it. I didn't.' Max's accusation was the last straw, and the injustice of it finally snapped Jess's sorely tried patience. She cried angrily, 'Those two came on board with their cutlasses between their teeth, and they made straight for me. I tried to head them off, but it didn't work. The only thing I could do was to hit back. The only language they understand is their own, and if they don't like it being used against them, that's their fault, not mine. I won't allow anyone to walk over me in such a roughshod manner.'

'They were my guests.'

'Then they should behave in a manner befitting guests.'

'As my future wife, I expect...'

'Don't I have a right to expect something, too?' Jess flared. 'Like common courtesy, for instance? I'm your future wife, not your bond servant. And if I'm to be mistress of Blythe Castle——' jeering, she hurled his own words back in his face '—if I'm to be mistress of Blythe Castle, I intend to be treated as just that. I won't be set aside as a nonentity by either your guests or your staff. You can't have it both ways, Max,' she rushed on as he opened his mouth to speak. 'You might as well make up your mind to that. If you insist upon taking me for your wife, I won't accept half-measures. If you don't like the idea, then set me free.'

'Neither will I accept half-measures, Jess.'

The glint in his eyes picked up her words, and moulded them into a very different meaning, and Jess gasped as his hands reached out and jerked her towards him.

'I don't accept half-measures in anything,' he grated, and poured out his fury in the savage intensity of his kiss.

His mouth was an angry demand that was a threat of even greater demands to come, and Jess quivered under its lash, and knew with a growing despair that if he chose to renege on his agreement to the marriage being in name only, she would be as helpless to resist those future demands as she was against the angry strength that pinioned her now.

When the storm was spent, Max thrust her aside and strode out of the room. With the slam of the door still vibrating in her ears, Jess's knees gave way. She sank on to the rug in front of the fire and buried her face in her hands, shaking as if with an ague.

Bob's prediction that they would have little time to spare during the next two days proved to be only too accurate. Jess saw nothing more of the Vaughan family. Whether or not Max contacted them, she did not know, and did not ask.

She had enough to do to attend to other visitors who came to the castle in increasing numbers, bearing wedding gifts. Most of them, she reckoned, came out of curiosity, since word that the role of leading lady had changed in the drama being enacted at the castle must have reached far and wide by now. But in the face of Max's haughty lack of any kind of explanation, and her own stoic silence on the subject, one and all were obliged to depart with their curiosity unsatisfied.

As the wedding gifts began to accumulate, Jess's sense of unreality grew. In an unbelievably short space of time, her whole life had been turned upside-down, and soon it would be changed for ever.

Max sent the estate secretary to help her to list the wedding presents, which continued to flow unabated until Jess felt bewilderedly as if they would soon need a whole new castle in which to house them.

Huw proved to be a cheerful young Welshman who was confined to a wheelchair, but whose brilliant organising abilities made nought of his paralysed legs. It transpired that he was an ex-jockey who had been disabled in a riding accident, and, talking to him, Jess learned that several more staff members suffered disabilities of one kind or another, but happily reached their potential doing satisfying jobs around the estate, which pointed to a wide compassion on Max's part that Jess would not have suspected of him.

She commented upon it at dinner on the Tuesday night, and Max answered offhandedly, 'I employ them because they're good at their jobs, not from pity. No one in their right senses wants pity.'

Certainly he showed none to Jess when they parted company that night with the wedding now just short hours away. Any last hope that she entertained that he might even at this late hour relent and set her free, died when he warned her, 'If you've got any silly ideas about running away, the same as Lucy did, forget them. Because if you do, I'll find you, Jess, wherever you are, and however long it takes.'

The next morning, Jess descended the stairs on feet as leaden as her heart.

The maid helped her to don her wedding finery, and this time Jess was unable to refuse her services because the girl came to her room armed with the message, 'Mr Max said I was to come and help you, miss.'

She settled the lace veil on Jess's head to complete the bridal outfit, and stood back to admire the picture she had helped to create.

'My, but you do look lovely, miss.'

Jess turned indifferent eyes on the mirror, not because she wanted to see what she looked like, but because it was expected of her. The hazel eyes looking back at her were the darkest she had ever seen them, almost black with the same shadows that had lain in Lucy's eyes so short a time before, under the same lace head-dress, but she, Jess, had not Lucy's avenue of escape open to her.

When she reached the drawing-room to await her escort to the church, she was nonplussed to find that Max was still there. He pivoted away from the window as she came in, and his eyes fired at the sight of her, but before he could speak Jess blurted out,

'I thought you'd be gone by now.'

'I wanted to make sure you hadn't,' he replied significantly, and turned as the door opened again to admit the stable manager.

'Hey, it's supposed to be unlucky for the bridegroom to see the bride in her wedding dress before the ceremony,' Bob teased.

'Max has already seen the dress on its hanger anyhow, so it doesn't matter,' said Jess dully.

One more bad omen could make little difference now, she thought hopelessly.

'I prefer to see the dress on you. You look lovely,' Max complimented her unexpectedly, and, opening a long, slender box, he lifted out a rope of perfectly matched pearls. 'The dress only lacks these,' he said, and reaching round Jess's neck he snapped the clasp closed.

Like a halter, to hold her captive. The pearls rested against the rich ivory silk of the dress, like the tears which Jess felt too numb to shed. When the clasp was fastened to his satisfaction Max kept his hands round her, his fingers tightened convulsively on her shoulders as if he would pull her to him, and he muttered in a voice that sounded strangely unlike his own, 'Jess...'

'If you don't come right away, Max, you'll be late at the church.' The best man stuck his head round the doorway. 'That's the bride's privilege, not yours. I don't blame you for not wanting to leave her, though, even for a minute.' He grinned, his merry eyes appreciating the dainty picture she made.

'OK, I'm coming.' Whatever Max had been about to say was lost, and he spun on his heel and followed his best man out of the door, and Jess gripped her tongue between her teeth to prevent it from calling him back.

The ordeal of walking into church today would be a thousand times worse than it had been on Sunday morning, and suddenly, irrationally, she needed Max's strength beside her.

True, Bob Tempest would be with her, but even the kindly Irishman was no substitute for the commanding personality of his employer, one which contrarily Jess needed now to help her through the ceremony, into which that same personality had driven her in the first place, against her will.

The bouquet of carnations and lilies began to tremble in her hands.

'Come now.' Bob took the flowers from her, and held on to her hand. 'I'll carry this to the car for you. It's time to follow on.' The stable jargon fell naturally from lips which smiled at Jess encouragingly. 'Sure, and the old castle's never seen a lovelier bride in all its history.'

The soft Irish voice, with its blend of gentleness and firmness, had the same soothing effect upon Jess that it had on Bob's four-footed charges, and although her mind did not register his actual words her feet somehow found the strength to obey him.

Panic rooted them to the ground when she descended from the limousine at the church gate, however.

Lilacs swung heavy on the light breeze, vying with the bridal white of wild may to load the sunwarmed air with perfume, but Jess saw only the sea of faces pressing forward, several deep along every inch of the narrow path to the church door, their owners unable to squeeze themselves into the too-small church for the ceremony, but determined not to miss a view of the squire's bride.

'Now you know how a filly feels on its first day at a race meeting,' Bob teased, and sent a nervous laugh shivering through Jess's lips, that gave the clapping crowd quite the reverse impression of her real feelings as she took her bouquet in one hand, and the stable manager's arm with the other, and felt grateful for the camouflage of the veil's heavy lace to hide her ashen cheeks from view.

'With this ring, I thee wed...'

The words sounded like a knell in Jess's ears, the deep barrel ring an intolerable weight upon her slender finger as Max slipped it neatly into place.

It gleamed, a golden mockery, in the bright sunlight that filtered through the lovely stained-glass windows as, the service over, Max turned her towards him. Lifting back her veil from her face, he exercised his right as her husband, and kissed her full on the lips in front of the watching congregation.

Jess held herself rigid to receive the traditional salutation, and the tears which had lain very close to the surface during the ceremony nearly spilled over at its unexpected gentleness.

Until now, the kisses she had received from Max had been hard, demanding and angry. This one was the very essence of tenderness, and it penetrated her guard with the subtle stealth of a ray of sunshine opening up the petals of a flower that had been tightly closed against an icy wind.

Did he delude himself that he was kissing Lucy? Intuition answered no. This was a seeking kiss, exploring uncharted territory. Unhurriedly his lips continued their journey, and for a long, heart-stopping moment, the time and the place and the people receded, and Jess was aware only of Max and the overpowering waves of feeling that washed over her, from the magnetic contact with his lips.

Stray thoughts wandered across her bemused mind. If Max was doing this for the benefit of the congregation, he was a superb actor. If she had not known better, she, as well as the watching wedding guests, might have been taken in by the reality of his performance.

If he kissed her, Jess, in this way, how would he kiss a woman whom he really loved? What would it be like, to be that woman?

Lucy must know. She, Jess, would never know, and the lack was an emptiness inside her during the hours that followed. She smiled for the photographers, responded mechanically to the congratulations of the guests at the reception, and for her pride's sake she pretended a brittle gaiety she was far from feeling, while she longed for a quiet corner into which she might escape and be on her own, if only for a few minutes, to enable her to recover from the effect of Max's caress.

His first kiss as her husband had disturbed her more than she wanted to admit, and she could not help but wonder if he would show the same gentleness towards her afterwards. If he would remember his part of their bargain...

Someone thrust a knife into her hand, jerking her back to her surroundings, and a merry voice demanded that she cut the first slice of the wedding cake. The cake that, if all had gone as planned, Lucy would be cutting instead.

Numbly Jess put the blade to the icing, but the sweet decoration was hard and resisted the ineffectual thrust of her nerveless fingers. Max came to her rescue, and put both his own hands over hers to help her. They closed round her wrists, trapping them, and Jess felt the muscles of her arms go weak as the knife cut deep and applause broke out among the guests; she felt as if the blade had turned in her own heart instead.

Someone put a glass of champagne into her one hand, and a plate containing a slice of the dark, rick cake in the other. She took a hurried mouthful of the wine to ease the agony inside her, but instead it made her feel dizzy, so that momentarily she leaned against Max to support her.

His voice in her ear provided a harsh astringent that steadied her more effectively than any wine could do.

'Why didn't you have something to eat, for goodness' sake, before you had a drink? You might know the stuff would go straight to your head. You haven't touched a mouthful of food since breakfast.'

Since dinner last night, but Max was not to know that.

'Food would choke me.'

'Risk it, and swallow some,' he commanded her callously. 'I don't fancy carrying an unconscious bride over the threshold.'

If he did, it would provide an answer to the question that was bothering her, at least for tonight, Jess thought raggedly.

Later that evening she danced in his arms at the ball which followed the reception, and wished that the music might never end, because each new tune brought the time inexorably closer when she and Max would be alone together for the first time as man and wife, and she would discover the answer for herself.

The last waltz was a memory. Max closed the door on the final, departing guest and turned to Jess, and his voice sounded hoarse as he reached out for her and muttered, 'Jess, I...'

In his eyes was the same elusive expression that had been there when he'd kissed her in the church, the same growing, flaring light, and it panicked Jess into urgent speech.

'I... You...' She got no further. Max took a step towards her, and her nerve broke. Clutching her dress in both hands to prevent its long ivory folds from tangling with her feet, she fled for the stairs.

His eyes followed her, she could feel them like twin beams piercing her back. He called after her, 'I'll come up when I've checked the doors,' and his words echoed like a threat in her ears as she stumbled towards the landing.

Without thinking, Jess made for the guest bedroom, but realised her mistake when she saw from the doorway that the cupboards had been emptied of her clothes, and the bed stripped. The sight jolted her heart into a hammering pain inside her.

With trembling legs she turned to follow her belongings into the master bedroom which Mrs Kirk had informed her that morning had been prepared a short distance along the corridor.

She wished there were a thousand doors in the castle for Max to check. Anything to delay him coming upstairs. She saw that the large double bed was made up for two, but that might be an automatic assumption on the part of the housekeeper, and have nothing to do with anything which Max himself had ordered.

Nervously Jess paced the room, but after half a dozen turns exhaustion from the long day overtook her, and warned her that she could not remain in her wedding gown all night.

With hands that shook, she slipped on the dainty nightdress, and covered it with a matching, floor-length robe which disguised its revealing lace, and made her feel ever so slightly better.

She did not notice Max when he first came into the room. Her every heightened sense was alert for the possibility of the door opening from out of the corridor, but instead he came in through an inside door, which linked his dressing-room with the main bedroom.

Jess sat at the dressing-table, nervously punishing her hair with a brush, and his bare feet made no sound on the thick carpet, so that suddenly he was behind her, his tall form filling the mirror.

The brush in her hand froze, and her eyes, enormous in her white face, stared into his through the glass.

Max, too, was wearing a robe, Jess saw, and sucked in a difficult breath. His robe was black, with gold and scarlet dragons woven into the silk, and their fiery breath was reflected in his eyes as he reached down and pulled her to her feet in front of him.

'You're beautiful, Jess. Did anybody ever tell you?' he murmured.

'Yes... No...'

'You're beautiful. And you're my wife.'

He bent his head, and his hair made a dark halo in front of her eyes, blotting out the room as he devoured her trembling mouth. An aeon of time passed before he drew back, and then only to bend and lift her high into his arms, and turn towards the bed.

'No, Max. *No!* You promised...'

Fear blinded Jess to caution. With frantic hands she pushed against him. He looked down into her upturned face, his mouth hovering once more close and closer above her own, and she threw up her hands to shield her lips from another assault.

'You little vixen.'

With a muttered oath Max jerked his head back, as the stone of her engagement ring caught sharply against the point of his chin. He put exploring fingertips to his face, and drew them away stained the colour of the ruby that proclaimed her as his.

'Max, I'm sorry. I didn't mean to...'

She hated Max, but she did not want to hurt him. With mounting terror, out of all proportion to the trivial nature of the scratch, she watched the thin line of it slowly darken.

It showed up the more clearly against the sudden pallor that whitened his face under its healthy tan, and his expression was a mask of fury as he glowered back at her.

Jess shrank away from the fierce blaze of his eyes.

'There's no need to cower,' he snarled. 'I won't hit you back, although goodness knows you deserve it.'

With contemptuous arms, he tossed her bodily on to the double coverlet that awaited their wedding night.

'Go to bed. Like we agreed, you can have it all to yourself. I don't take an unwilling woman. Not even my lawful wedded wife.'

In two long strides he crossed the room, and left Jess crumpled on the coverlet, too shocked to cry as the door of his dressing-room slammed shut between them.

CHAPTER FOUR

THE next morning, Jess grasped at the prospect of a ride to afford her raw nerves some relief.

Max did not appear at breakfast time, and, after a frugal mouthful of toast and coffee, she made for the stables. The casual wear she had made for Lucy she judged to be too tightly fitting for comfort in the saddle, so she resorted to the contents of her battered suitcase, and ignored Mrs Kirk's disapproving stare at the worn state of her jeans and trainers as she headed out of doors.

Max was lunging the stallion when she reached the paddocks. She could see his tall, upright figure, with his back turned towards her, standing in the centre of a wide circle worn by trotting hoofs, and hear his deep voice talking soothingly to the horse as he put it through its paces.

The picture they made stayed her feet.

The grey had a beautiful movement, and it held her fascinated to watch, but Max sensed her presence behind him. The moment she leaned her arms along the fence, he turned his head, and seeing her there he immediately checked the horse and sent it trotting in her direction, allowing him to turn his own body round to face her.

Their glances locked across the width of the paddock and Jess caught her breath, feeling as if she was held on a leash by his stare, in the same way that he held the stallion on the rope attached to its head leathers.

'Walk on,' Max commanded firmly as the horse slowed its pace, and incredibly Jess felt her own limbs respond to the order. She straightened up from the fence and stepped out, and thought, this is crazy. I'm not here to obey Max's every command, the same as his horses.

She walked on nevertheless, driven by the compulsion of his following stare that made her feet stumble in their haste to take her out of its range. Behind her, she heard Max call out sharply, 'Jess,' but this time she had herself under better control, and she continued walking, ignoring his command, and the call was not repeated.

Instead, after what seemed an endless silence, her straining ears caught again the sound of equine command. 'Steady. Whoa.' And then again, 'Walk on,' and the tension that knotted the muscles in her shoulders against the intrusion of those gimlet eyes slowly released itself. Unconsciously, as she reached the stable block, and the building hid her from Max's sight, Jess put up her hand to massage away the ache left in the back of her neck.

Bob was crossing the yard, and called out to her cheerfully, 'I didn't expect you today. I thought you'd be too tired, after yesterday.'

'I came along for a ride, to blow the cobwebs away.'

What the stable staff thought of Max coming down to the stables without her, and immediately resuming his training of the stallion the day after their wedding, she neither knew nor cared. Bob showed no curiosity at the odd behaviour of the newly married couple, and simply said, 'Max has put aside a couple of mounts for you to choose from. But come and see the new foal first.'

The stable manager could not have chosen a happier distraction, more capable of taking Jess's mind off the tensions of the previous twenty-four hours, and she asked eagerly, 'A new foal? When did it arrive?'

'Very late indeed, last night,' Bob returned ruefully. 'They always seem to chose a time that gets me out of bed. In here,' he guided her, and held open a door.

'Here' proved to be a large tack-room, and Jess looked askance at its lack of animal life.

'You can see the foal from here, on closed circuit television,' Bob explained. 'It saves us having to go into the foaling box each time we want to check up on progress.' He indicated a screen placed unobtrusively in a corner, and smiled at Jess's cry of delight as she caught sight of the spindly-legged newcomer nuzzling its mother's flank.

'You seem to have all the space-age equipment to help you,' Jess admired the efficient-looking set-up.

Bob nodded. 'There's a specially designed peephole, too, with a wide-angle lens fixed into the door, so that we can keep a close eye on what's going on. That way, unless the mare is having difficulty, we don't need to disturb her at all until the foal actually arrives.'

'When can I go inside and see them?' Jess begged, unable to restrain her eagerness.

'You can come in now, with me,' Max said from behind her. Jess spun round with a gasp, and the look of delight drained from her face.

'It'll disturb the mare,' she objected instantly, hanging back.

'Not now the foal's arrived. He's already several hours old, and he has to get used to seeing human beings around him. Come.'

Max took Jess by the elbow and propelled her forward, and perforce she had to go with him or risk a scene in front of the stable manager.

'He's a little beauty, isn't he?' Max's admiration was unfeigned as he paused with Jess to inspect the new-comer. 'You've done very well,' he congratulated the mare, as she dropped her nose towards his pocket and was not disappointed when he rewarded her with the expected sugar lump.

Would he have rewarded *her* in the same patronising manner if she had been more accommodating last night? Jess wondered cynically, but on this subject at least she could not help but agree with Max.

'He's beautiful,' she breathed, and her hands reached out towards the foal.

Instantly she checked the gesture, but the objection she half expected from Max did not materialise. Instead he remarked, 'You can fuss him if you want to. The sooner he gets used to being handled, the better. Physical contact helps to build up trust.'

'Maybe it does, in horses,' Jess flashed, and saw from the sudden tightening of Max's jaw that the significance of her shot was not lost upon him.

'The mare's getting restive. It's time to go.'

He punished her by denying her a longer stay with the foal and, being no expert with horses herself, Jess could not argue with him, although she could detect no sign of distress in the mare.

'I've put those two mounts for Jess in the loose-box at the end of the row,' Bob said when they returned to the tack-room, and he turned to accompany them along the wide walkway between the stables, stopping where two long heads appeared over neighbouring loose-box doors, to greet their approach. 'They'll both give you a nice gentle ride,' he promised.

'I think I'd better start on the smaller one,' Jess said cautiously. 'I've only ever ridden a pony before, and that not very often, and the other horse is much taller.'

The height of the second animal was intimidating, and Jess had no desire to fall off and make a fool of herself on her first ride.

'I'm coming with you on Cloud, so you'll have to ride the other one,' Max said, instantly reversing her decision.

'I'll go and get the tackle ready,' said Bob mildly.

Jess's eyes snapped. Max was insufferable. He must
think it amusing to try to frighten her by insisting that
she rode the taller of the two horses. There could be no
other reason for him to insist upon the change, just because he wanted to come along with her on Cloud.

She took in an angry breath to argue.

'Oh, there you are, Max. I've brought my sulky along
for some practice on the track. Be a darling and time
me, will you?'

Nina! Jess glowered as the girl approached them across
the stable yard. She was faultlessly dressed in jodphurs
and a blue roll-necked sweater that enhanced the colour
of her eyes, and made Jess instantly conscious of her
own shabby appearance. Anger stirred in her at the other
girl's effrontery.

In her world, one did not call another woman's
husband 'darling' in quite that provocative tone of voice,
and, unable to help herself, Jess rose to the challenge
with a snapped, 'Max is riding with me.'

'Riding?' The rising question was a sneer. Thinly
plucked eyebrows rose, and the blue eyes underneath
them swept over Jess's jeans and trainers. 'Surely not,
in that gear?'

Jess went scarlet, and then white, as Max butted in,
'I'll do better than time you. I'll give you a race, if you
like.'

'What about our ride?' Jess burst out angrily.

She did not want to have Max ride with her, she would
have made every effort to avoid having his company, but
equally she had no intention of allowing Nina Vaughan
to walk in and demand his attention as if she, Jess, did
not exist.

'Best to leave riding until you're properly kitted out,'
Max answered. 'You'll be more comfortable in jodphurs
and boots.'

'I'm sorry I didn't come fully equipped with bowler hat and hunting pink,' Jess snapped, and thought savagely, the piece of equipment I'd most like right now is a riding crop, to teach Nina better manners.

Max answered imperturbably, 'It wouldn't be any use here if you had. I don't allow hunting on my land. You can watch us race instead, for today.'

He turned away and called across to a stable lad to come and help him harness the sulky. Nina cast Jess a triumphant look over her shoulder as she followed him, tapping a victory roll against the top of her highly polished boot with the end of her riding cane.

Jess watched with angry eyes as the two sulkies rolled on to the track together.

'I thought I heard Miss Vaughan's voice,' Bob commented as he came to join her.

'Nina and Max are supposed to be racing the sulkies,' Jess said shortly.

Even to her untutored eyes it did not look much like a race. The two vehicles circled the track at a leisurely pace, travelling in tandem, so close together that their drivers might as well have been sat in the same vehicle.

Jess saw Nina turn and say something to Max, and heard the rumble of his deep voice in reply. They were too far away for her to hear the actual words, but Nina's light laugh floated back to her like a taunt.

Bob glanced at her set face and explained quietly, 'They're pacing the first circuit. They'll begin to race the second time round.'

The two sulkies swung back to the starting point, still in tight formation, and then Max called out, 'Three, two, one...now!' and the two horses stretched into their traces.

It was exhilarating to watch. Still trotting, the animals reached a speed which Jess would not have thought possible without them having to break into a gallop. She had watched harness racing on television often enough, but seeing it live for the first time, at such close quarters, was altogether different.

'Going at that speed, it's a wonder they don't gallop,' she exclaimed.

'They'd be disqualified if they did,' explained Bob. 'If they break gait on the track in a race, they have to pull to one side and regain it before they're allowed to continue.'

'It can't be easy, holding them to a trot.'

'It takes skill on the part of the driver, and a lot of training for the horse. The excitement of competing gets through to the animals as well as to the humans, and it's instinctive for them to want to forge ahead of the rest of the herd.'

The excitement was communicating itself to Jess. Although it was not a race in the official sense of the word, Jess found herself fiercely willing Max to win. She longed to shout and stamp, urge him on, and the sheer primitive ferocity of her reaction shocked her, so that she was hardly aware of Bob speaking, until she felt his hand on her arm.

'As you're not riding today, why not come and try driving instead?' he repeated. 'It isn't difficult to learn for someone who already knows how to ride. Let's get some tack, and harness up the small mare.'

Bob acceded to her request to use the smaller of the two animals, if Max did not, and silently Jess turned away from the rails, and followed him back to the tackroom. She watched as he selected a set of leathers, explaining the exaggerated length of the reins with, 'For the first few times, it's best to walk behind the horse, driving it at a walking pace, just to get the feel of things. Then, when you've done that once or twice, and you

feel confident, you can put the horse to a sulky, and
really drive.'

Jess nodded, and surreptitiously rubbed the palms of
her hands down the legs of her jeans. The unexpected
upsurge of emotion as she watched Max and Nina racing
against each other had left the palms of her hands
clammy.

Bob's quick eye caught the movement.

'It doesn't do to show fear when you're handling
horses, particularly thoroughbreds.'

'I'm not afraid. A bit nervous, perhaps.' Jess could
not explain the real reason to the stable manager.

'Nerves, excitement, call it what you like, it all sets
the adrenalin flowing, and that comes through as fear
to the horse. It's liable to make the animal play up, so
just to be on the safe side I'll rub a bit of this ointment
on you.'

He reached up and hooked a tub of something from
the tack-room shelf.

'What is it?' Jess asked without any particular interest.

'A horse aromatic. It masks the scent of adrenalin
which makes the horse think you're afraid of it. Just
knowing that you're wearing it will probably make you
feel more confident, so that you won't really need it
anyway. And if that isn't Irish, I don't know what is.'
He smiled, and drew an answering laugh from Jess as
she stood still to allow him to rub a little of the cream
on her forehead and hands.

'My, my. It looks as if you've just got back in time,
Max.' Nina's tinkling laugh grated on Jess's taut nerves
as they came into the stable yard together, and signally
failed to turn the barbed remark into a joke.

Nobody else laughed. Jess jerked away from Bob's
attentions, and the stable manager frowned, but his voice
was evenly quiet as he answered, 'As Jess isn't riding

today, it seemed a good idea for her to have a lesson in driving instead. Naturally she's a bit nervous, it being her first time.'

Max said nothing, but there was a brooding question in the look he turned on Jess which fanned the coals of her resentment to white heat. Before the growing flames could find expression, Nina turned to Max with a smile.

'Thanks for the race, Max. I'll be back for another one soon. I'll need lots of practice before the County Show. My horse doesn't stand a chance of winning against Cloud, but it should come in a good second. Pity about your ride,' she added sweetly to Jess, and quit the yard with a satisfied smile on her face that reminded Jess of a cat that had just stolen the cream.

A member of the stable staff cut across the uncomfortable silence that followed her departure with a message for Bob. 'A delivery of potash has just come in, Mr Tempest. Where do you want it stored?'

'You go ahead and attend to the lorry driver, Bob. I'll give Jess her first driving lesson.'

The dark look on Max's face suggested that the lesson might be on another subject than driving, and Jess lashed out in self-defence the moment Bob and the stable man were out of earshot, and before Max had an opportunity to speak.

'Nina Vaughan shouldn't judge other people by her own questionable standards. How dare she suggest...'

'Nina wasn't suggesting anything. Surely you could see that she was only joking?'

'Some joke. She was the only one who seemed to find it funny.'

'You're imagining things.' So was Max, Jess thought tartly, if his set expression was anything to go by, but before she could say anything he accused, 'You're simply prejudiced against the Vaughans.'

'I'm nothing of the kind. I don't like Nina any more than she likes me.'

'Neither of you has got any valid reason to dislike the other.'

How little Max knew! Jess stared at him incredulously. He himself was the reason for their mutual dislike, and she was astonished that his conceit seemed to be completely unaware of it. She declined to point it out and boost his already inflated ego, and he gave her no opportunity, by sweeping on. 'Forget Nina, and let's get on with your driving lesson.'

Fervently Jess wished that she could forget Nina, and as if by magic found her wish granted when Max put the reins into her fingers, and, stationing himself immediately behind her, so close that she could feel the hard length of him pressing along her spine, he put an arm on either side of her, and covered her hands on the reins with his own.

His lean wrists, whipcord strong from constant use of the lunging ropes and reins, were like steel bars hemming her in, as he commanded, 'Walk on,' and obediently the horse started forward.

Perforce Jess had to do the same with Max against her back, forcing her on. His closeness was unnerving. The light astringent smell of his aftershave lotion enveloped her from behind, mixed tantalisingly with the faint male scent caused by the exertion of his work-out with the stallion, and the sensuous combination of the two startled Jess's heart into a swift, uneven tempo which sent the blood racing through her veins, and made her eardrums throb.

Max was like his stallion, dangerous. Jess felt her own essential femininity respond with a swiftness that was both a shock and a warning, and she wondered confusedly if the aromatic cream would work to mask her reaction from the man, as well as from the horse.

The palms of her hands felt slippery on the reins, and tingles of fire inched along the length of her spine. To extinguish them she pressed back against their source, and humiliation coloured her cheeks when Max commanded her instantly, 'Don't lean back, or you'll pull on the horse's mouth. Lean forward, and guide it lightly, as you will when you're driving a sulky.'

At least on the seat of the sulky she would be on her own, and Jess wondered bewilderedly why that should seem suddenly less attractive than it had a few short minutes ago.

The rest of the lesson passed in a daze. Her every nerve vibrated with an intense awareness of Max, making it impossible for her to concentrate on his instructions, and she smarted under his impatient, 'For goodness' sake, pay attention, or you'll never learn.'

Only instinct from her early riding lessons saved her from complete disaster, and she grasped at the excuse of Bob's return, with some papers for Max to sign, to end the torture and make her escape back to the house.

Her reprieve was short-lived, however. At lunch Max told her, 'I'm going into town this afternoon. Come with me and get your riding kit, and I'll arrange for you to have an account opened at the big store there.'

'I don't want an account.'

'You'll need clothes.'

'Those I've got are more than enough.'

'Maybe for now, but they won't be for very long.'

Jess did not intend to remain with Max for any longer than she could help, certainly not for long enough to wear out the large trousseau she had made for Lucy, but she could not point that out to Max.

Last night warned her that she must foreshorten the time as his wife as much as she possibly could. She could not trust his forbearance to continue, and the consequences if it broke would be catastrophic for her.

'I've got some money of my own. If I need something special I can get the material, and make it up for myself.'

The amount of money she had left was pitifully small, but her independent spirit revolted at being totally dependent upon Max.

'You won't have time for dressmaking.'

'Time?' Jess eyed him in astonishment. 'That's the one thing I have got plenty of. There's nothing whatsoever for me to do in the house. It's all run like clockwork between Mrs Kirk and the cook, and I can't spend all day, every day, in the stables.'

'That will soon alter,' Max predicted, and Jess wondered uneasily, did he mean to alter it himself, by filling a nursery to occupy her time?

Tight-lipped, she remained silent, and he said harshly, 'Don't be stubborn, Jess. As my wife, I intend to provide you with all your needs.'

Bitter experience had taught her that it was a waste of breath to argue with him. She shrugged. She would take the credit card, and simply not use it.

She forced a smile, however, when the manager of the exclusive store in the centre of the nearby market town welcomed them both effusively that afternoon.

It was the class of store which Lucy had patronised when choosing materials for her trousseau, and Jess made a mental reservation to travel further afield if she was obliged to make a purchase, because her dwindling capital would be as a drop in the ocean here.

'If you'll just sign here, Lady Blythe, underneath your husband's signature, I can let you have your card for use right away.'

At first Jess did not realise that the manager had spoken to her. The title bounced off her unaccustomed ears, and Max touched her arm to draw her attention as the man repeated his request.

'Lady Blythe...?'

'Of course. I'm sorry. I was daydreaming.'

'Thinking about your shopping list, no doubt,' the man mistook her inattention.

Jess met the glint of derision in Max's quick glance, and knew the sour taste of defeat as she took the pen held out to her, and bent over the form to sign on the dotted line.

Not only must she accustom herself to one unwanted name, she must get used to being called by two.

It took a physical effort to drive her fingers to form the words, Margaret Jess Beaumont, underneath the strong pen strokes that promised Maxwell Jonathan Beaumont would guarantee all his wife's future expenditure in this emporium.

With all my worldly goods, I thee endow...

She did not want the worldly goods, or their owner, and as she straightened up from the bitter task Jess refused to meet what she knew must be triumph in her husband's eyes at this further victory.

There would be others which she must endure before she could be free, but not, she vowed, the one which would give Max the ultimate power over her.

She forced a dry, 'Very,' when the store manager commented, 'How appropriate that you both have the same initials,' and accepted the store's credit card from his hand with reluctant fingers.

Max said, 'You must christen it at the perfume counter,' and scored again, because Jess was unable to refuse when the manager insisted upon accompanying them to introduce her to the floor supervisor, thereby making sure his distinguished new customer would be instantly recognised on any future visit to the store.

Feeling suddenly stifled by the attention, Jess made one last attempt to extricate herself.

'I only use the cruelty-free perfumes. The ones that have not been tested on animals,' she declared forthrightly. Perhaps the message of compassion had not reached this far into the countryside yet?

The manager's bright smile grounded her ill-aimed missile. 'We've got a very wide stock of those products to choose from. Indeed, they're fast outselling the old-fashioned perfumes, now people have become aware of how they are tested. One accepts the need for medical research, of course, but in the pursuit of elegance, the sophisticated modern woman demands assurance that it isn't based on suffering.'

His super-efficient exterior cloaked a very human heart, and Jess warmed to the store manager, which salved her pride somewhat when she hesitated over the choice of two perfumes, and Max insisted, 'Have both,' thus doubling the charge on her new credit card, which she had promised herself she would not use at all.

It was the same with her riding kit, which alike would be charged to her account. Max commented, 'My wife hasn't ridden since she came to England, so she'll need a complete kit to use right away, while her other is being tailored.' And he helped her to choose chocolate-brown jodphurs and a finely woven hacking jacket, 'to go on with'.

'I hope you'll find our garments meet the very high standards you're accustomed to, Lady Blythe.' The manager's eyes openly admired the suit she was wearing, and there was a hint of anxiety in his voice as he questioned delicately, 'Paris, perhaps?'

Sternly Jess repressed an urge to laugh in his face. Holding on to her gravity as best she could, she enlightened him, 'On the contrary. I design and make all my own clothes.'

Perhaps here might be the very opportunity she needed to start selling her work locally. Her hopes rose as high as the manager's eyebrows as he ejaculated, 'I would have staked my professional reputation...' He broke off, and his expression became eager. 'I must say, Lady Blythe, you have a quite remarkable talent. Many of the top-class fashion houses who supply us with clothes would give a great deal to find a designer of your calibre.'

It was the lifeline she needed, and Jess reached forward to grab it, but Max got there first.

'My wife doesn't have the time to accept commissions,' he said curtly, and the manager quickly about-faced.

'Of course not. Naturally, I was joking.'

He had not been joking, and Jess knew it, so did Max, but he slew the idea at a stroke, and Jess hated him with a burning ferocity mixed with mounting despair.

The manager would talk about this, word would get round the small market town and filter out into the surrounding countryside, and any hope she might entertain of finding an outlet for her skills within a fifty-mile radius of the castle would be stillborn. She felt helplessly as if she was drowning, and Max was standing on the shore and callously chopping off at source any ropes thrown out to rescue her.

To her vexation he remained with her while she was being measured for more jodphurs and jackets, and the moment the tape measure had done its work she tugged her skirt back into place, confusedly aware of the laughing appreciation in Max's eyes that mocked her warm cheeks, while appreciating the tapering grace of her limbs, that would show off her new riding clothes to perfection.

Their next visit was to the local bank.

They walked together through the afternoon bustle of the streets, which effectively checked the angry condemnation which Jess longed to hurl at Max's arrogant head. She tried to remain outside the door when they reached the building, and leave Max to go in alone, but he insisted, 'You must come with me, to give them a sample of your signature.'

'Why should they want my signature? I don't intend to transfer my own money here.'

His look was steely. 'I've arranged for a regular monthly allowance to be paid in here, for you to use as you need it. They've probably finished the formalities by now, and will have your cheque-book and first statement ready for you.'

This was heaping coals of fire with a vengeance, and Jess's scorched pride forced an angry disclaimer through her clenched teeth.

'I don't want your money. I've told you, I won't take it.'

'You can't refuse.' In the seclusion of the entrance lobby Max turned on her, and his face was tight. 'You agreed to be my wife...'

'You blackmailed me into becoming your wife.'

'...and as Lady Blythe, you'll be involved in things which will need money. You can't come to me each time to ask for petty cash.'

'I wouldn't ask you for a single penny.'

'Having an account of your own will save you the trouble.'

It was like facing a tank with a barricade of matchsticks. Max overrode her objections as if they did not exist, and once again Jess had to steel herself to sign her new name. She nearly choked over the cup of tea provided for them in the manager's office when she read the figure on the statement which he handed to her along with her new cheque-book.

Its size inflamed her anger to boiling point. Max was not missing a single opportunity to rub salt into the wounds which he himself had inflicted, and the bitter irony of having at her disposal more money than she had ever owned in her life before—Max's money—and not being able to use it to gain her freedom from him, turned her tea to vinegar. Pride would allow her to use only her own money for that purpose.

The moment they were alone again in the car together, she rounded on him.

'What you've put into my account isn't petty cash. You must know that I can't possibly have a use for such a huge sum of money every month.' A gnawing ache deep inside her made her voice raw as she rushed on, 'Don't think you can bribe me to change my mind about our marriage. Money and possessions don't grab me. Neither does a title.'

'I never imagined they did. Call the allowance working expenses for the job, and if you still think it's too much in six months' time, we'll discuss it again then.'

In six months' time Jess hoped fervently that she would not need his money at all, and for quite another reason, but his tone closed the subject, and she was content to let it pass until it reopened itself at dinner time without any prompting from her.

When they sat down at table, Jess found a small pile of post neatly stacked beside her plate. 'Who can be writing to me?' she wondered out loud. 'I don't know anybody here.'

'You won't know them, but they'll know you,' Max answered, and commenced to slit open his own similar pile, leaving Jess to answer her own question.

The first envelope she opened requested a donation from Lady Blythe to a well-known charity.

The second one invited Lady Blythe to open a local fête in aid of church funds, 'and to remain afterwards to grace the occasion with my presence,' she read out loud with an irrepressible gurgle of amusement.

Max looked up from his reading, and his eyes soaked up the laughter in hers. 'What did I tell you? If you accept even half of the invitations that come your way, you won't have a minute to yourself.'

He had meant she would be occupied with public duties, and not in the castle nursery. Relief flooded through Jess, and she veiled her eyes with her lashes to hide it, saying decisively, 'I've never opened a fête in my life, and I don't intend to start now.'

'It's part of the bargain.' Remorselessly Max held her to the letter of it. 'As my wife...'

'As your wife,' she mocked him bitterly, and his brows drew together.

'As Lady Blythe, if you like it better that way.'

'I don't like either, and you know it. In any case, why should they ask me to open their functions? I've only just come on the scene. Surely there must be other people who have done the job for them before? Regulars, from the local community?'

'I've done what I could up until now, and Kate Vaughan has taken over one or two things like fêtes and so on, which are more the province of the ladies, because there hasn't been a lady at the castle for a good many years, until now. That will all be altered from now on.'

Not for any longer than she could help, but in the meantime... Jess frowned down at the invitation. Max had driven her into a corner, but she might yet be able to use it to her own advantage.

Kate Vaughan would not easily relinquish her position of local patroness, even though that position was a delegated one, and great would be her triumph if Jess refused to occupy her rightful place in the local society. Which meant opening things like fêtes.

'I'll think about it,' Jess compromised, unwilling to capitulate without at least a show of independence, and turned her attention to the other envelopes in the pile.

Max enquired casually, 'Is there anything else interesting among your lot? Mine are all business letters, mostly about the stables.'

'This one wants me to present prizes at the school speech day, and the children's hospital in the town want me to open their new ward. The rest are more requests for donations. What shall I do about those?'

Now Jess saw the reason for the size of her monthly allowance, and the account at the local store. She saw something else, too, with growing clarity. As Lady Blythe, she would be regarded locally as a public figure, which meant that her eventual break with Max would swiftly become public property, too, making her plan to slip away when the time came without any fuss out of the question.

Max must somehow have guessed this, and was deliberately trying to tighten his hold upon her. Jess picked at her dinner without appetite as he answered, 'Accept the invitations you feel you can cope with. They'll help you to get to know the local people. But don't allow all your time to be taken up. I want most of it for myself.'

His peremptory tone was a reminder of his power over her. Jess flushed and accused him sharply, 'You didn't tell me anything about the public side of being your wife.'

He shrugged off her thrust. 'Having a title carries a lot of responsibilities, and absolutely no perks. Just remember that you belong first to me, and not to the world at large.'

'I'm my own person. I'm nobody's property,' Jess flashed, and ducked his retaliation by rushing on, 'Anyhow, you haven't answered my question. What shall I do about the donations? How much...?'

How much would she be expected to give? Jess had not the remotest idea and, however much it grated, she was forced to turn to Max for guidance.

'You can discuss those with Huw. He's got his finger on the pulse of these things, and will suggest appropriate amounts to give. And if you indicate "yes" or "no" on the invitations you receive, he'll reply to them for you as well, and keep a diary the same as he does for me. I'll instruct him to make sure we both have adequate free time to ourselves.'

He calmly reasserted his hold on the reins, and snubbed them tight when dinner was over by deciding for them both, 'We'll get through some of the thank-you letters for the wedding presents this evening, while things are quiet. There won't be much time once the preparations for the County Show start.'

'You write the letters. I don't know the people. They're your relatives and friends.'

'*Our* relatives and friends. Our marriage makes us one.'

Not if she could help it. Jess drew in a ragged breath as his thumb massaged tantalisingly up and down the top of her spine, arching her towards him.

Her head tipped back in response to the sensuous stroking, exposing the slender column of her throat to seeking lips that keyed the tender pulse spots into urgent, throbbing life.

A tiny moan escaped her parted lips, and it triggered off an instant response from Max. Before the sound had time to die away, Jess found herself crushed in a breath-expelling embrace that took her unawares, and gave her no time to erect any defences against it.

His lips trailed fire from her eyes down to the wildly throbbing hollow at the base of her throat, setting her veins alight, and her body bent in a bow of instinctive response under the ardour of his caress.

This was worse, much worse, than when he had kissed her in church. Terrified as much by her own reaction as by his, Jess twisted her head from side to side to try to free her lips, and managed to disengage them for long enough to mumble, '. . . in name only. That doesn't include being kissed.'

He lifted his head then. 'Our marriage has got to appear normal to outsiders.'

'There aren't any outsiders around to see us now.'

'So, practice makes perfect.'

Twin devils in his eyes suggested that he was enjoying his practice more than somewhat, and, against all reason, Jess discovered to her utter consternation that she was beginning to enjoy it as well.

'I... You...' Her tingling lips stumbled over the words, and the devils danced more wildly still. Suddenly she was unable to watch them, and dropped her lashes to cover her confusion, aware that the tide of colour flooding her throat and cheeks must print her feelings like a book for him to read.

'You...what?' he murmured, tipping up her chin with a firm hand, forcing her to look up again, into his laughing face which mocked her distress.

'I...' A discreet knock on the door saved her from more. A maid entered and with tactfully averted eyes put down the tray of after-dinner coffee on a nearby occasional table. Jess sank into a chair and began to pour out with trembling hands, betraying her need for the dark, scalding beverage to steady her shaken nerves.

'Thank you, Ellen.' Max offered the courtesy that her closed throat could not, and turned to busy himself with glasses at the sideboard. They exchanged beverages, and Jess sipped at her glass cautiously, but even so the fiery liquid it contained stung her throat, making her cough, and adding to the heat of the fire which raged through her veins, threatening to burn her up.

Max was doing this to soften her up, to make her compliant to his wishes. To establish trust, on the same principle that he applied to the foal. Jess knew a bleak emptiness that he was not doing it for love, and scorned herself for it, and for her own response which she was helpless to prevent, and which traitorously urged her to exchange kiss for kiss.

But no matter how often Max kissed her she would never trust him, never naïvely come to him as, one day, the foal would come, and eat out of his hand.

Apprehensively she prepared for bed at the end of the evening, fearful that Max's earlier ardour might return and tempt him to break his bargain, and carry his practice further.

Tensely Jess waited, her knees hunched up to her chin, a slight, forlorn figure in the middle of the large bed. Max remained downstairs to address the last few letters, ready to give them to Huw for franking in the estate office the next morning, and Jess's ears strained for the sound of his footsteps coming upstairs.

When at last they began to ascend they hesitated outside the landing door and she froze, but after what seemed an endless pause they passed on, and Jess heard the door of Max's dressing-room open and shut.

But it was not until the thin thread of light under the adjoining door finally snapped into darkness that weariness overtook her and she dropped into a troubled sleep, oblivious, as she cried out against her dreams, of that door opening, and a pair of strong arms reaching out to smooth the bedclothes that were tumbled by her tossing, while silk dragons waited patiently on the bed beside her until the nightmare was spent, and she breathed quietly in their protecting embrace.

CHAPTER FIVE

THE next morning, more post arrived for Jess, following the same pattern as before.

She gave the pile of invitations a slightly harassed look, and Max reassured her, 'You won't get quite so many in the winter months. During the summer, most of the fund-raising committees try to hold outdoor events while the weather's good, but afterwards there's only an occasional charity ball, so it isn't quite so hectic.'

By the winter Jess hoped to be long gone, but with an effort she restrained her thoughts and merely said, 'They're all good causes. I shall feel guilty if I go to some and refuse others.'

'If you do refuse, they'll simply ask someone else, probably Kate Vaughan.'

Being the second bead on the string would not please the redoubtable Kate, thought Jess drily, as Max continued, 'You'll have to learn to say no to some of them. You can't be in two places at once. Anyway, put them aside for now. You can see Huw about them when we get back from York. Today is our day off. It's the last one I'm likely to get until after the County Show is over, and we can have a proper honeymoon.'

The irony of it wrenched from Jess a bitter, 'Ours isn't a proper marriage, so why pretend?'

'Whose fault is that?' Max snapped; he meant one thing, and Jess meant another, and her face went white.

'I've parked the Range Rover outside, Max.' Bob Tempest strolled on to the terrace outside the open french windows of the breakfast-room, and prevented a return volley. 'Morning, Jess,' he greeted her cheerily. 'It's a lovely day for your ride out.'

He tossed the Range Rover keys across to Max, who fielded them neatly and answered, 'I hope we can find something worthwhile to bring back from the auction.'

With a wave of his hand Bob turned to retrace his steps. 'I'll keep my fingers crossed for you,' he called over his shoulder.

'Why don't you take Bob with you to York, instead of me?' Jess said hurriedly to Max before the stable manager could go out of sight. 'This sort of thing is more in his line than mine.'

'Anything that's in my line is in yours from now on. Have you ever been to York?'

His abrupt question checked her angry denial, and instead ejected a surprised, 'No, why?' from her lips.

Lack of funds had obliged Jess to confine her sight-seeing up to now to the admittedly rich hunting ground of the capital, and the cathedral cities had had to remain an unfulfilled ambition.

'Then for goodness' sake stop fighting, and let's enjoy at least one day together in reasonable harmony.'

To Jess's surprise, she discovered that she *was* enjoying herself. They had breakfasted early, and as they set off the sun shone; the high-riding vehicle enabled her to see over the hedges and across wide views of the countryside, its fields still wet with dew, that would have been obscured from the low-slung Jaguar.

As the miles rolled behind them, Max entertained her with tales of other forays he had made in search of cast-aside sulkies that could be restored to racing condition.

He proved to be an excellent raconteur, and in spite of herself Jess was soon laughing freely at his account of the various salesroom tactics to which eager buyers were wont to resort to obtain their desired bargains, and the struggles he and Bob had between them overcome, in order to get his prizes back home.

In a shorter time than seemed possible, they reached the outlying areas of York, and skirted the city to reach the countryside beyond, and the farm they were seeking.

It lay on a high, windy plateau that would be bleak in the winter months, Jess guessed, and surprised herself by comparing the site unfavourably with the gentler countryside surrounding Blythe Castle.

They turned off the road along a track, and as they approached the granite farm buildings Jess saw the paraphernalia of work on the land, lined up for inspection by the people who had come to view.

Men in tweeds and corduroys milled about the outdoor implements discussing the merits and demerits of each particular piece, while their womenfolk did likewise with the household equipment, and a sudden depression seized Jess. The accumulation of a man's lifetime was being mercilessly exposed to an uncaring audience, and she felt suddenly like a trespasser on its late owner's privacy.

Not quite all uncaring, she discovered. Max surveyed the cloud on her face, and tuned into her thoughts with quick perception. 'The farmer would have wanted his tools to be used, rather than let them lie and rot,' he said quietly.

'It all seems so... so...' Jess choked on her ability to find words to express feelings she could not begin to analyse.

'These things happen. I believe the holding has been in the hands of the same family for generations, but the last owner died a bachelor. It must have been a burden to the old farmer, to realise that there would be no one left to carry on after him,' he added reflectively.

Had shades of that same burden driven Max to take a wife, any wife, in place of the girl who had jilted him?

It seemed unlikely. He cared little enough for his title,
and there were others in his family to carry on the line,
but the possibility was a disturbing one, nevertheless,
and the weight of its unease sharpened Jess's reply.

'Nothing can be a greater burden than a loveless
marriage.'

They were back to square one. The brief rapport of
the journey was shattered, and Jess regarded the shards
with uncaring eyes. Their temporary truce had altered
nothing, but she flinched from the look which Max directed at her as he opened his mouth to reply.

'We'll take Lot Four first, ladies and gentlemen, and
get it out of the way, so we'll have a bit more room to
move about.' The auctioneer's call cut off whatever Max
was about to say, and stilled the clatter of conversation
going on around them.

Lot Four was a very large and unwieldy-looking farm
implement, with gadgets that stuck out at awkward
angles, catching at people's feet and clothing as they
moved among the exhibits, and good-natured grumbles
from the milling crowd had prodded the auctioneer into
action earlier than the time stated on the catalogue.

The bidding was brisk, and the implement was soon
knocked down at a good price to a burly young farmer,
who hitched it to his Land Rover and towed it away to
relieved cheers, while the auctioneer cautioned, 'Bidding
for the rest starts in half an hour, folks, so if you want
something, be here.'

The half-hour had to be filled in somehow. The eddy-
ing of the crowd carried Max and Jess along with it, and
they came to where the sulky was parked, its dilapidated
state drawing a smaller complement of viewers than the
farm implements.

Jess paused in front of it, but Max promptly tucked
her arm through his and urged her forward. 'Keep

moving, but slowly. Don't show too much interest.' They circled the sulky and, with Max's arm drawing her closely against him, Jess could feel the tension in his tall frame, like a terrier quivering at the scent of its quarry.

Max coveted the sulky. Why, Jess could not imagine. To her eyes it looked neglected and broken down; it was covered in dust and cobwebs, and seemed to be irre-deemable. But Max's outwardly casual glance had taken in all he wanted to know, and it must have told him that the vehicle was capable of being restored and put back on to the race-track where it belonged.

Jess glanced up into his face. It was impassive, showing no interest, but she could feel the excitement of the chase rising in him. It was infectious, catching at her imagin-ation, and suddenly she wanted the sulky, too, for Max.

She could feel herself echoing his shudder as a broad Yorkshire voice behind them said, 'The buggy'd be useful, with a box top nailed on to it. It'd be right handy for carting sacks of fertiliser.'

'Sacrilege,' Jess whispered, tipping up her face to Max, and his eyes brimmed with laughter, chasing away the storm clouds, while his arm tightened round her own in a conspiratoral hug.

The rapport was back, and a strange thrill pierced Jess as they walked on together under the shelter of a large Dutch barn that held the furniture and various household items.

Two women were arguing over a large oak sideboard. 'I could do with that, to hold my bits and pieces,' declared one, but the younger of the two protested, 'It must weigh a ton, Mother. How will you get to move it, to clean behind? Why don't you have some-thing nice and new instead, that won't be so heavy to shift?' The speaker cast a disparaging eye on the rest of the furniture on display. 'There's nothing else here that isn't as heavy as the sideboard. The bits and pieces look as if they're mostly junk.'

'I don't suppose Amos ever got round to having a turn-out. A man alone doesn't bother with things, not like when he's got a woman.'

The two passed on, but their words remained like an echo of desolation in Jess's ears. A man alone. Max would be a man alone, after she left him.

But Max was different. Max was hard and self-sufficient, and would wrest from life whatever he wanted, regardless of what it might cost other people.

The thought stiffened her away from him, and immediately his eyes lanced downwards on to the top of her head, feeling her withdrawal, but Jess kept her face averted and pretended an interest in what the younger woman had described as junk.

It was the flotsam and jetsam of long-forgotten family life. A hobby-horse with no mane, and one wheel missing, was draped with a child's skipping rope, the once brightly painted wooden handles chipped and faded, the bells rusted beyond repair, and the centre of the rope worn almost through with long ago energetic use.

'Let's go back. It's almost time for the auction to begin,' Max urged.

'No, wait for just a moment.'

Jess's quick eye espied a trunk full of old toys. The lid was raised, and the top of the trunk was littered with battered teddy bears and various soft toys, the stuffing exposed by the ravages of generations of moths, and various parts of their anatomy missing.

Underneath the stuffed toys... Jess caught her breath. The papier mâché face of a small boy doll looked up at her appealingly, and craning forward she could see what looked like other dolls beneath it.

'I'd love that trunk of dolls,' she pleaded.

Max looked astonished. 'What do you want dolls for?' His eyes suddenly kindled in a penetrating question. 'Thinking of the future?' he teased.

Jess flushed. She was, indeed, thinking of the future, but not in the way Max visualised it. Carefully she controlled her rising excitement.

'Maybe,' she prevaricated. 'I'd like to dress them.'

'You could buy new dolls, with ready made clothes.'

'It wouldn't be the same. Please, Max. You get fun out of restoring your sulkies. Don't deny me the same pleasure in restoring the dolls.'

She struck a bull's-eye there and knew it, and watched with mounting satisfaction as Max nodded thoughtful agreement. 'I hadn't looked at it quite like that.'

'I must have a hobby,' Jess urged craftily. 'Now that I'm not dressmaking any longer, it doesn't mean that I've lost my interest in sewing. I can't cease to be the person I was, just because I'm married. Dressing dolls would be the perfect pastime.'

'You shall have them if you really want them. I suppose you could always give them away to one of the sale-of-work stalls at the fêtes.'

Giving the dolls away was the reverse of what Jess had in mind, and she hid her glee with difficulty. If her eyes had not deceived her, and the trunk contained more of the kind of doll she had glimpsed half-hidden by the jumble of soft toys, once they were restored and redressed they would sell for a very high price. Enough to fund her for a while when the time came for her to leave Max.

Part of Jess's college course had been the study of dress through the ages, and the beautifully costumed dolls on display in various collections had aroused her

interest, so that she had continued her research long after
the need for it was gone.

She found the dolls themselves as fascinating as their
costumes, and the glimpse of the one in the trunk was
enough to tell her that it was probably eighteenth century.
If her guess was even nearly correct, and the rest of the
toy was in the same excellent state of preservation as its
head, it was a collector's item of considerable value.

It was Jess's turn now to urge Max away to where the
auctioneer had set up his stand, and he laughed indul-
gently at her undisguised haste, teasing, 'Before you
know where you are, you'll be hooked by the collecting
bug as well, and be bidding on your own account.

'You bid for me. I don't know how. I've never been
to an auction before.'

She had difficulty in containing her impatience as the
farm equipment came under the hammer, gaining the
prior attention of the auctioneer as befitted the assumption of male superiority, Jess thought cynically; the
household furniture came next.

The middle-aged woman had evidently heeded her
daughter's advice, and the sideboard and its companion
pieces were knocked down to a keen-faced man who,
from his appearance, was not one of the locals.

'He's a dealer in antiques,' Max told her *sotto voce*,
and Jess felt herself go cold. A dealer? Would he recognise the doll for what she was certain it was worth, and
outbid Max for it?

Not knowing its value, Max would not be inclined to
bid very much for what he, too, probably regarded as
junk, and if she revealed to him what she suspected about
the trunkful of old toys, it would be as good as con-
fessing her intentions, and enough to make Max refuse
to bid for her at all.

In a quandary, Jess bit her lip. She remembered her ex-landlady telling her that dealers cleared houses *en bloc* in the hope of striking occasional gold in the form of precious paintings and such like artefacts, stored away in attics and forgotten by their owners.

Was she about to stand by and see yet another lifeline snatched away from her before she could grasp its end and pull herself to freedom? Desperately she hoped that Bob Tempest would remember his promise and keep all his fingers crossed for her, as well as for Max.

The bidding continued apace. The main items of machinery went quickly, and the sulky came next under the hammer. Max looked down at her, and his eyes said, 'Wish me luck'; surreptitiously she raised her own crossed fingers for him to see.

His eyes warmed on her face for a brief, breath-stopping moment, and she blamed the sudden erratic behaviour of her pulse on the excitement of the chase as the auctioneer began his patter. Max withdrew his gaze from her face, and fixed it unswervingly on the speaker.

Why did Max not call out, if he wanted the sulky so much? Jess wondered, puzzled by his unaccountable silence. Others were bidding steadily and the price was rising. And then she noticed that every now and then Max raised his catalogue slightly, just enough to catch the alert glance of the auctioneer.

Others in the crowd, she noticed, were employing similar tactics, but one by one the bidders dropped out as the price rose higher, until only three seemed to be left. One was the dealer, bidding against Max, and a younger man who stood a few feet from them among the crowd.

The atmosphere became tense as the price continued to rise, and Jess's nerves tightened in sympathy. Every ounce of her willed Max to win. Why she should care, she knew not, but the silent duelling between the three men caught at her imagination, as the bidding rose to what she considered astronomical levels for the sulky, which from its condition she had regarded as fit for little other than kindling.

At last, with a shrug, the dealer dropped out, and at the next bid so did Max's final rival, and the auctioneer brought down his gavel with a sharp crack.

'Going to the gentleman on my left. Going, going...gone!'

The sulky belonged to Max.

Jess felt a silly desire to laugh and cry at the same time, and her eyes were bright with excitement as they signalled her feelings to Max. She caught an elusive something in his downwards glance that raised her excitement to fever-pitch, and dropped her eyes away from his in sudden confusion.

'Congratulations,' the younger man called out to Max, clearly without animosity.

'You beat me to it at the last sale,' Max called back, 'so we're quits. See you on the track.'

'I'll be there to take my revenge,' his rival promised.

Max explained to Jess, 'He's a member of the National Harness Racing Club, too. He'll be at Blythe, racing his team at the County Show. After this, I'll warrant he'll give me a hard fight for the cup.'

The cup that meant so much to Max this year, in order to establish the supremacy of his stallion. A sense of apprehension seized Jess, and it must have shown on her face because Max smiled down at her and said, 'Don't worry, it'll be a fair fight. The Club comes down very severely on any attempt at foul play, and that man's a clean driver, and a good sportsman.'

He fell silent as the auctioneer called again, 'Now for the residue, ladies and gentlemen, and then we can all go and have our lunch,' drawing the attention of the onlookers back to the rest of the business in hand.

The crowd had thinned considerably. Most of the men were already gone, their interest in the heavy machinery having been served, but Jess saw with dismay that the keen-faced dealer remained.

Was he *au fait* with the world of antique dolls?

He bought several old clocks, one of which clanged a discordant protest at being carried away from its former home, and the tight knot that settled in Jess's stomach made her feel physically sick as the auctioneer finally started on the odds and ends, which included the trunk of toys.

The dealer bid steadily, and soon he and Max were the only two calling the tune. The irony of watching Max battling to purchase the means to fund her own freedom from him struck Jess forcibly, but her glee at outwitting him was tempered by anxiety as she watched the dealer with strained eyes. Would he go above what Max would reckon to be a fair price for a trunk full of oddments?

She held her breath until it became a painful stitch in her side, and let it out in a gasp of pure relief as the man gave up just when Jess began to fear that Max might do the same.

The dealer's particular forte was furniture. His van was already full to overflowing, and his stomach felt distinctly empty. He looked at his watch, and the hour decided him. If the fellow who bought the sulky wanted the trunk full of old toys, then good luck to him. The contents looked to be of no use for anything but the dustbin, and the trunk itself wouldn't sell for very much anyway, people weren't going for that sort of thing these days.

'To the gentleman on my left. Going, going . . . gone!'

'Oh, Max, thank you.'

The relief from the almost unbearable tension rocked Jess off balance. It did strange things to her head, and even stranger things to her self-control. In an excess of delight, she threw her arms round Max and hugged him.

'If it has this effect on you,' he grinned, 'I'll buy you a trunk full of old dolls every day.' He hugged her back, to the open amusement of the onlookers nearby. But the wide smile on his face brought Jess down to earth with a rush.

In the excitement of battling for the dolls, she had almost forgotten the reason why she had wanted them in the first place. Memory returned, and she hurriedly extricated herself from Max's arms with the scarlet-faced excuse, 'Let me go. People are staring.'

'Let them stare.' But he released her good-humouredly and said, 'Let's get the sulky on the roof-rack, and we can sling the trunk of toys in the back of the car.'

'You'll do nothing of the kind,' Jess protested indignantly. 'You'll handle them carefully. I don't want my dolls broken.'

'If they were, would you cry?'

His laughing look offered comfort if she did, and a quiver ran through Jess. She thrust it away impatiently, because it should not be there now that the excitement of the auction was over.

'I'll help you to lift the sulky,' she returned hastily, but Max refused.

'It's too heavy for you. I'll manage.'

'I'll help your man, lass,' offered a burly bystander, and together he and Max secured the sulky on to the roof-rack.

Jess watched anxiously as they turned to pick up the trunk of dolls between them. She longed to scream at them to be careful, and Max threw her a taunting look, seeing her tension, but he slid the trunk smoothly enough into the back of the Range Rover, with never a bump to endanger the fragile contents.

Jess went limp with relief as he tossed a rug over the top to cover it from view, and locked the door securely behind it. Her fingers itched to empty the trunk and examine the toys more closely, and it took all her will-power to restrain herself from having a peep at them there and then.

With a huge effort of self-control she managed to desist, and smiled her thanks to the volunteer helper as she got into the front seat beside Max without so much as a backwards glance at her precious acquisition. She must not allow Max to suspect that he had just handed her the key to her eventual freedom, for fear that he might once again find some means to wrest it from her grasp.

The euphoria of her success remained with her throughout their visit to York. They had a late lunch at a hotel that came straight from the pages of a Dickens' novel, and afterwards walked off their meal along the city's ancient walls.

The beauty of the Minster awed them to solemnity, and Max explained to her the details of the restoration work still being undertaken to make good the ravages of the lightning-induced fire.

Out into the sunshine again, they chased away the gravity with a fascinating game of 'I-spy' as they sought out the old craft signs sited among the narrow shopping streets, mostly fixed at top-storey level which kept their eyes craning upwards, reading the streets like the lines of a book of days gone by. Max knew the city well, and under his expert guidance Jess soon became adept at spotting yet another unique landmark, and they ended in the narrow, cobbled gulley of The Shambles, laughing, and counting their score.

Afterwards, Max insisted upon taking Jess on a breezy river-boat in order to show her the city from the water. She demurred. 'Oughtn't we to be getting home?'

She spoke without thinking, and suddenly became aware of two things at once. Unconsciously she had referred to Blythe Castle, for the first time, as home. And Max's quick mind had latched on to the word, and brought his eyes swiftly to rake her upturned face. The grey pools held a look that made her heart race, and this time she could not blame it on the excitement of the auction.

Her pulses throbbed to his touch as he took her by the arm and helped her on to the river-boat, and her unquiet thoughts found no reassurance in his casual reply. 'There's no haste. It's our day off, remember?'

She fell silent when they returned to the car park and climbed back into the Range Rover, and she grasped gladly at the excuse when Max asked her, 'Are you tired?'

'Mm. A little. It's been quite a day.'

'There'll be more, but not until after the County Show is over.'

Not then, if her hopes in the trunk were realised. To save herself from having to reply, Jess gave in to Max's suggestion without protest when he said, 'Close your eyes, and have a nap on the way back.'

But, however tightly she pressed her lids together, they were no defence against her disturbed thoughts, nor, she discovered uneasily, could they shut out the subject of them.

Every slight movement Max made was transmitted by her heightened sensitivity with the clarity of a radar beam, making her as vividly aware of him in the seat beside her as if her eyes were opened and watching him.

The faint astringent scent of his aftershave lotion made a clear link with her nostrils, and her quick ears made another as they followed each slight movement of his body when he manipulated the vehicle controls, and the two together chained her to him with a bond that dispensed with the need for sight.

Her nerve-ends stretched instinctively, reaching out towards him as a flower reaches towards the sun, and, no matter how she argued in silent desperation that it was a purely physical attraction, the chemistry between them could not be denied. It would need only one small spark to ignite the mixture into an explosion.

Max was her husband, but he must not become her lover. Fear made Jess's lids fly open again, and she saw with growing dismay that, to prevent her fears from being realised, she would now have to fight herself as well as him.

Back at the castle, the gardener conveyed her precious trunk to the small guest bedroom where her sewing machine still stood, and Max made no protest when she suggested tentatively, 'I could turn the room into a hobby room, then I can do my sewing at odd moments without having to tidy everything away again each time.'

It would also serve the purpose of keeping the dolls away from potentially knowledgeable eyes, if chance visitors should arrive while she was working on them, but Jess had to restrain her impatience to examine her purchase for a little while longer when Max said, 'I've got to take the sulky down to the stables to unload, and I want to drop in at the estate office to give Huw the bill of sale. Come with me, and bring your invitations for him to deal with.'

To refuse might arouse his curiosity as to why she was so exceptionally eager to look at the dolls, so Jess collected the morning post without comment, and smiled at Bob's jubilant reception of the sulky when they reached the stable yard.

In an odd sort of way, Jess felt as if it was her sulky, too, because she had stood by during the bidding and willed Max to win it.

'I'll get the wheelwright on it first thing tomorrow,' the stable manager enthused, probing the new acquisition with a sharp pointed tool. 'One or two of the spokes are loose, but the wood itself is quite sound.'

'The barn where it had been kept was dry. I checked.'

The two men discussed technicalities, and Jess's attention strayed to what looked like a large pile of planks dumped at the side of the race-track that had not been there yesterday.

'The stands for the Show were delivered this morning,' Bob answered her enquiring look, and added, 'Miss Vaughan has arranged for the erectors to start work on them right away.'

'Nina?' Jess swivelled a questioning look at Max, who enlightened her.

'Nina's on the organising committee of the Show. Part of her responsibilities will be to attend to the overall layout of the site.'

Nina would probably use that as an excuse to practically take up residence at the castle until the Show was over, Jess predicted sourly, and was justified soon afterwards when they went to the estate office to see Huw, and found Nina sat on the edge of the secretary's desk, swinging her legs.

Hanging round on the off-chance of bumping into Max, Jess judged, as Huw looked up with a carefully blank expression on his face, and greeted them with, 'How did you get on at the auction?'

Max answered enthusiastically, 'We got the sulky. I've just unloaded it in the yard. Here's the bill of sale, to put through the books.'

Although Max probably spoke without thinking, the 'we' sent a strange thrill of pleasure running through Jess, that evaporated when Nina jumped from the desk and clapped her hands, and cried, 'Oh, Max, I'm so pleased for you.'

She'll start jumping up and down next, Jess thought disgustedly, but Nina demanded instead, 'I must try it out on the track. Now. Right away.'

'Nobody must use it until it's been properly restored, and I'm sure that it's safe to drive.' Max did not suggest when that might be, nor promise to allow Nina to try out the buggy then, a lack which surprised Jess, but Nina persisted.

'Take me to see it. I can't wait.'

She thrust out her hand in the direction of Max's coat sleeve, as if she was about to tug him towards the door that minute, but Max demurred. 'It'd be a shame to spoil your pretty dress. The sulky's covered in dust and cobwebs. So am I, after handling it.'

Smilingly he held out his grubbied hands palm outwards towards Nina, and the movement effectively stopped her in her tracks. Her dress was powder-blue broderie anglaise, to match her eyes, and the slightest mark was bound to show. Although Max had dusted off his hands on a stable rubber, they were still in a condition to leave distinct prints on anything so delicate.

Jess restrained a smile with difficulty as Nina drew back, nonplussed, and Max continued, 'We only came down to bring the bill of sale to Huw, and some odds and ends from the morning post. Did you bring your invitations, Jess?'

'Invitations? Already?' Nina exclaimed sharply, as Jess handed over the clip of papers to Huw.

She ignored Nina's probing, and spoke directly to Huw. 'The top few are invitations, and the rest are requests for donations to charity.'

'I'll deal with the donations, and let you have the letters and cheques for signature some time tomorrow.' Huw leafed through the invitations quickly. 'There's no need to reply to these right away, except for the one to open the local fête. That's being held quite soon, and the organisers will need to know your decision in case you refuse, and they have to ask someone else to open it in your place.'

'There must be some mistake.' Nina's face reddened. 'Mother always opens the local fête. She's done it for years, because there's been no Lady Blythe at the castle.'

'There is now,' Jess reminded her, and made up her mind quite suddenly. 'Will you accept that invitation for me, please, Huw? I'll let you know my decision about the others when I see you tomorrow.'

'Certainly, Lady Blythe.'

Did Huw use her title deliberately? He was not usually so very formal. Jess could not be sure, but his words flicked Nina's already high colour to a richer hue, and Jess thought she detected the trace of a twinkle in the Welshman's eyes which cheered her as she turned to follow Max outside.

This was carrying the war into the enemy's camp with a vengeance, but she felt no qualms of conscience, and trained her guns on Max instead when he turned on her as soon as they were in the Range Rover together.

'Did you have to rub it in so hard with Nina? She's bound to feel bad that her mother has to take second place at the premier local "do".'

'I doubt if Nina's got any feeling for anybody, except herself.'

'Nina wouldn't hurt a fly.'

'Only if she thought the fly wasn't big enough to hurt back. Now she's discovered that I am, and will, it might make her a bit more wary of crossing swords with me in future. Anyway, you told me to accept the local invitations so that I could get to know the people.'

'You're prejudiced against the Vaughans.' Max rejected her excuse as petty.

'If you think Nina's such a paragon, why didn't you marry her instead of me?' Goaded, Jess struck back, and flinched when Max retaliated,

'Don't make me wish I had.'

If her luck held, Max would soon have his wish granted, Jess fumed as she escaped to where her sewing machine still stood in the small guest bedroom.

The trunk of toys had been placed on the floor beside it. She dropped to her knees and lifted up the lid, and delved into the depths. The soft toys she slipped into a plastic sack for disposal later, and gently lifted out the small boy doll which had first attracted her attention.

The papier mâché head was crazed with minute lines, but was otherwise well preserved, and its sweetly grave expression drew a reluctant answering smile from Jess's lips.

If the rest of the doll was in the same excellent state of preservation as its head ... Hardly daring to look for fear that moths might have made inroads into the body, Jess set aside the crumbling uniform of some long ago proud regiment, and could not restrain a cry of satisfaction as her probing fingers met a fine, very soft leather body underneath, and wooden arms and legs.

There was nothing here to attract moths, and her own nimble fingers would soon recreate the uniform from the pattern of the old one; she could use the local reference library to obtain details of appropriate regimental colours where these had faded beyond recall.

Jess sat back on her heels feeling slightly dizzy.

Boy dolls of that era were a rarity in themselves, and to discover one in this condition was a find indeed. Once restored, it should be worth a lot of money. This was a stroke of luck beyond her wildest dreams, and she put the toy aside carefully, and delved into the trunk again.

Among a clutter of bric-a-brac it disgorged three more dolls. They were all girl dolls this time, but all, she saw gleefully, were of superb quality. One had the much sought after Bru mark on its head and body, and that, too, was in perfect condition, although the bisque head of the next doll was broken in one place, sufficiently to erode its market value as a collector's piece.

The third doll was not a toy at all, Jess saw, but a Pandora, a two-foot high model once carried by travellers from the French fashion houses to advertise their latest styles, before the days of common reading skills and freely available newspapers and magazines in which to advertise their wares made the use of model dolls redundant.

Jess stroked the elaborate gown, each tiny pin-tuck carefully stitched into place by some long forgotten fingers, and wondered what connection a French fashion house could have with an isolated Yorkshire farm.

Even the small dolls were toys for only the very wealthy of their period. Had some long ago farmer so doted on a child that he was prepared to break the thrifty habits of a lifetime and spend freely on toys for his spoilt darling?

Or, more likely, had the daughter of a local wealthy family been married off to the farmer, perhaps against her will, and taken her childhood belongings with her to comfort her in the harsh environment of unaccustomed household chores? And, looking at the treasures of happier days, had the young bride longed to be free of the new, bleak world in which she'd found herself?

Soberly, Jess laid the dolls back in the trunk and shut the lid down on them. Restored and redressed, they would provide the means to fund her own freedom.

So why, instead of the triumph which she expected, did she feel this illogical urge to weep?

CHAPTER SIX

THE days that followed became increasingly busy, and Jess rarely saw Max alone for more than a few minutes at a time.

The pace of organising the County Show increased dramatically as the date for the opening drew closer. The man co-ordinating all the activity was a professional, who took the Show from venue to venue each year, and co-opted local help for his committee once the site had been decided upon. He gladly accepted Max's offer of accommodation at the castle and an office on the estate complex for the duration of the Show, and Jess welcomed his presence to ease the increasing sense of strain between herself and Max that had become unbearable since their quarrel.

True to his promise Max made no attempt to come to her room at night, and, as Jess watched the spear of light flick on and then flick off under the communicating door, the resulting blackness seemed to reach out and grip hold of her spirits, adding to her confusion and bewilderment.

Max went out of his way to avoid her, and she should have been glad, but instead found herself growing increasingly tense, which made her irritable when they did happen to be alone together.

It erupted one day when, under pressure from Max, Jess had spent an endless session packing up wedding photographs to send to the principal guests. Several of the addresses were missing from the list which he had given to her, and when she asked him for them, so that

she could post the packages that day, he brushed aside
her request with a brusque, 'Not now. I want to get the
show ring roped off this afternoon, so that Nina can
sort out where to put the jumps.'

Nina again. The girl was becoming part of the furniture. Under the guise of being a member of the committee, she did not miss a day coming to the castle, and
she waylaid Max at every opportunity, begging his help
with trivial details until Jess wondered angrily why she
bothered to be on the committee at all, since Max appeared to be doing most of the work.

She knew her attitude to be dog in the manger, when
she did not want Max herself, but she could not help it,
and, with nerves already rubbed raw by seeing her own
forced smile looking back at her from the wedding
photographs, she flared at him angrily, 'You asked me
to do the photographs so as to get them off in today's
post. How do you expect me to do that, without the
addresses?'

'Another day won't make any difference.'

'That wasn't the impression you gave me this morning.
From the way you pushed me into doing them, anyone
would think it was a matter of life or death.'

'I've got something more important to think about
this afternoon.'

His words suggested the show ring, but the searing
look he directed at Jess said, 'more important than you',
and a glacial cold invaded her as he turned on his heel
and strode from the room.

Max skipped lunch, and Jess, after eating alone and
without appetite, took herself along to the stables for
her now daily ritual of a visit to the new foal, much later
today because of the unwanted work with the wedding
photographs.

She discovered Nina and Max sitting on a pile of planks, talking and laughing, sharing sandwiches and coffee from a picnic basket which, from its size, was patently packed for two, and must have been prepared by Nina for that very purpose.

Furious anger melted the glacier inside Jess and left a raging, red-hot fire that scorched Nina's triumphant look as she hurried by them tight-lipped. Ignoring Max's call of 'Jess...' she made blindly for the tack-room.

Melted ice made rivers flow, and as Jess leaned back trembling against the closed door she put up exploring fingers to her face and was shocked to discover that her cheeks were wet.

She turned her anger against herself to dry them, and it put strength back into her shaking limbs, enabling them to carry her on into the foaling pen with her customary titbit for the mare, and a fuss for the foal.

The little creature was growing rapidly. She had heard Max discussing with Bob the possibility of turning it into a paddock with the other mares and foals quite soon, and the prospect added to the sense of desolation inside her. The foal had come to look forward to her gentle caresses, and trotted up to her fearlessly, encouraged by the dam's courting of the daily apple and sugar lump, but Jess knew that once it had other foals to romp with the link between them would be broken, and she would miss the contact more than the foal.

Her driving lessons, too, would come to an end when she left Max. Under Bob's guidance she had made rapid progress, and at his urging came to the stables for daily coaching.

'You'll learn in no time, if you do it regularly,' he encouraged her.

'Nina said it takes ages to learn.'

'That's for ordinary pupils. You're a natural. You've got hands.'

'Hands?' Jess surveyed her appendages quizzically.

'Horse-world jargon,' the stable manager grinned. 'Like green fingers for gardeners.'

By now Jess had graduated to driving a sulky, although she tried to take it out on the track only when Max and Nina were engaged elsewhere.

She was not always lucky, and today proved to be no exception. Under their critical stare she drove badly, and earned a sharp reproof from Max, who quit the stack of planks to come and lean against the track fence and watch her.

She drew up, and he said abruptly, 'I've told you before to lean forward slightly. The lines are there to guide the horse, not for you to hang on to as if they're a parachute harness.'

'Maybe a parachute would make her feel safer,' Nina gibed, and Jess writhed under her sarcastic laugh.

'Nina and I are going to have another practice race before we start on the show ring,' Max said. 'Watch us. Maybe you'll pick up a few tips.'

'I could pass on one or two,' Nina murmured with a provocative sideways look at Max that suggested her tips might not be about harness racing, and Jess fumed silently as she watched the two idle their sulkies on to the track a few minutes later.

'I thought you said you'd got more important things to do,' she flung at Max as he drew his horse to a halt beside where she stood against the fence.

'The cup race is crucially important for Cloud. The more practice he gets before the Show, the better.'

He drove on without another word, and Jess glowered as he caught up with Nina, and the two began to circle the track together.

Max allowed Nina to win the race, and Jess felt an urge to slap him for his indulgence of the spoilt girl. Nina blatantly showed off and her driving performance left much to be desired, but it did not earn the reproof from Max he had been quick to level at Jess, and she smarted at the contrast as she watched the contest that was no contest, with brooding eyes.

Cloud was capable of far greater speed than Max demanded of the stallion, Jess knew. She had watched him too often, racing round the track on his own in the early morning, not to notice the difference in performance now.

Watching Max had become another daily ritual while she visited the foal early each morning, before the work of the day had begun on the show ground, and long before Nina put in her daily appearance.

In the cool of the young hour, with only herself and his own stable staff around to see, Max was wont to let the stallion stretch itself to its full potential.

It was a thrilling sight to watch, as the perfectly matched racing team of man and horse spun round the track, the only sound the faint whirr of the sulky wheels on the track surface, accompanied by the brittle clip of the stallion's hooves, and an occasional lark swooping overhead.

Max did not carry a whip. He relied on his voice to control the horse, and it responded instantly to each quiet, familiar command from behind it. At the start of the home straight Jess would listen for the expected, 'Go!' from Max, and grip the rail with excitement as Cloud obediently leaned into his harness, and surged forward at racing speed to fly past her beside what would be the winning post in a race.

Now, racing Nina, the word was not spoken. The girl carried a whip, and used it to sting her horse to maximum effort, laughing immoderately as she sped past Max a full head in front of the stallion.

'That's the way to drive,' she jeered as she passed by Jess, and Jess turned away in disgust.

She did not want to drive like that. She wanted to drive as Max did, with her voice, and not with a whip, but her enthusiasm for his tactics waned that evening when he used words to drive her pitilessly instead.

The show organiser joined them at dinner, and as usual the conversation centred around the dramas and difficulties encountered during the day. The organiser smiled across the table at Jess, and acknowledged gratefully, 'At least I don't have to worry about persuading someone to open the Show for us this year. It's very good of you to take on the job, Lady Blythe.'

'Open the Show?' Jess choked on her spoonful of soup. 'I don't...'

'My wife doesn't mind in the least,' Max put in smoothly as the soup went down the wrong way, and a paroxysm of coughing seized Jess and effectively stifled her indignant denial.

By the time she got her breath back, the talk had moved on to other things. Jess fumed in silence during the rest of the meal, but rounded on Max over coffee later when the organiser was called away for a few minutes to take a telephone call.

'I didn't say I'd open the County Show.'

'The organiser asked me, and I agreed for you.'

'You've got absolutely no right to involve me without consulting me first.' Jess stared at him aghast. To open the local fête was quite bad enough. She had accepted that particular invitation on a wave of bravado, in order to put Nina in her place, and was already beginning to regret the impulse. Butterflies in the stomach was a mild description of how she felt each time she thought about

standing up on the vicarage lawn and making a speech
to anything of up to a couple of hundred local people.

To have to give the same performance in front of what
might well be an audience of several thousand at the
immense and hugely popular County Show filled her with
horror.

'As your husband, I've got every right.' Max remained completely unmoved by her anger.

'I can't do it. I won't,' Jess panicked furiously.

'You can't very well refuse. As the castle is hosting
the Show this year, it's the most natural thing for you
to perform the opening ceremony.'

'You criticised me for accepting the invitation to open
the local fête, so why...?'

'The fête will provide an excellent nursery slope for
you to practice on.'

Max broke off as their guest returned from taking his
telephone call, and asked him urbanely, 'Coffee? A
brandy, perhaps, to go with it?' He turned away, leaving
Jess to fill their guest's cup, while he performed the same
service for his glass at the sideboard.

Her contribution to the conversation that followed was
spasmodic. The men discussed the areas given over to
show jumping and the coming sheepdog trials, and where
to site the livestock pens, and the hundred or so stands
that would be required for the widely diverse firms to
whom the show was an annual magnet at which to ex-
hibit their wares.

Jess pretended to be absorbed in her hand-sewing, only
putting in an occasional remark when she was drawn
into the conversation by a direct question, her thoughts
grappling frantically with ways in which she might evade
this latest dilemma.

She was smocking a dress for one of the small dolls,
but, far from finding the task a soothing one, the mech-

anical action of working the coloured silks across the tightly gathered material allowed her troubled thoughts free rein.

It was cruel of Max to throw her in at the deep end like this. If one of them had to open the County Show, why could he not do it himself? He was using a whip on her, and mercilessly, such as he would never wield on his stallion.

Soon afterwards the vicar's wife joined them, and unwittingly added another dimension to the pressure Max had already exerted. Sally Venables was a middle-aged, cheerful, and very down-to-earth mother of three, and Jess liked her on sight. She was in charge of the large exhibition being staged by the various local craft organisations, and years of experience as a vicar's wife had taught her how best to get her own way.

'I need a marquee with at least an eight-foot frontage, on the most walked-past spot on the Show ground,' she declared without preamble, and the organiser threw up his hands in despair.

'Everyone wants the same. All the premier sites have already been let out to firms.'

'Then shove them up a few yards, to make room for mine. It's no good arguing,' she stopped him in midprotest. 'I need that spot, and I mean to have it. It's for an excellent cause. The craft organisations have all agreed to donate their work for sale on the last day to help fund the minibus used by the home for disabled children. It won't matter if the crowds have to walk a few yards further on to see the other exhibits. They'll all have two good legs. The children at the home haven't. Don't you agree, Lady Blythe?'

'I do indeed.' Jess nodded. 'And call me Jess.'

She was heartily sick of the title. It set her apart from other people, creating an artificial barrier just when she felt she most needed human warmth from somebody, for Max was deliberately keeping her at a distance, glee- fully widened by Nina at every opportunity.

'If you'll call me Sally.' Their visitor leaned over to touch the sewing lying on Jess's lap. 'That smocking is exquisite. What is it for?'

'A doll's dress,' Jess began, when Max interrupted.

'Didn't I say those dolls you bought at the auction would come in handy for one of the fêtes? They're just the thing for Sally's craft tent.'

'No!'

The refusal fairly exploded from Jess's lips. She could not allow Max, anyone, to wrest the dolls from her. They were her means of escape, and the one lifeline which Max could not chop off at source since he was as yet unaware of its significance.

Jess was conscious of three pairs of eyes beamed on her like so many searchlights. She felt herself go scarlet, and then white. Max looked angry, the organiser mildly surprised, and Sally frankly puzzled by her vehemence.

The latter said mildly, 'Of course, I wouldn't dream of pressing you to give them, if you'd rather not.'

'I can't,' Jess ground out, and her fingers dug on to the head of the small doll lying underneath the sewing on her lap. They found the broken portion of its head, and it was as if the small, inanimate thing was trying to give her a plausible reason for her refusal. She had de- liberately brought downstairs with her the doll that was broken, in case Max should ask to see what she was doing and, seeing the spoiled head, would lose interest, but now the broken head came into its own.

'I can't,' she repeated, steeling herself to speak more normally. 'When people pay money for something, they've got a right to expect it to be in good condition.

These dolls aren't. They're old, and this one's head is broken.'

She turned the doll round on her lap, sufficiently for the top of its head to show, and felt thankful that she had not yet found the time to glue back the missing bits. which still lay in the bottom of the trunk.

With a bit of luck, Sally Venables would not know anything about antique dolls, and Jess went on brightly, 'I've got a better suggestion. I'll buy some new dolls from the store in town, and dress them for you. There's still time between now and the Show. In fact, I'll go further, and do one for the fête as well if you like.' She managed what she hoped looked like a sentimental smile. 'I'd like to keep the broken ones myself. They're a souvenir of my very first auction, and my first visit to York.'

'I know how you feel.' Sally nodded. 'I've got lots of pieces of chipped china, with "a present from Blackpool" or wherever written all over them, and I wouldn't part with them for the world.'

Well satisfied with the organiser's resigned, 'I'm outnumbered. You shall have your marquee just where you want it', the vicar's wife took herself home shortly afterwards.

'See you at the fête on Saturday,' she called as she hurried away. 'Let's hope the weather holds.'

Jess waved her goodbye, and cravenly wished that it might pour with rain, and so reduce the crowds who attended, making her task of opening the function that much less nerve-racking.

True to her promise, however, she paid a visit to the store in town at the next opportunity, begging a lift from Huw when he had to go to the bank.

She used her credit card to purchase half a dozen dolls of various sizes, along with a supply of bright cotton print and ribbons with which to dress them.

The visit to the store jogged into life an idea which had been slowly taking root in her mind ever since she had first unearthed the Pandora doll from out of the depths of the trunk.

If dolls of similar height were decked out in the latest designer clothes, they would make a unique window display. The novelty would add to the attraction, and in the windows of a large London store such a display would draw extra attention to the styles in which the dolls were dressed.

Her own styles.

Immediately she returned to the castle, Jess used the excuse of having to dress a doll for the coming fête to lock herself in the newly designated sewing-room and put her idea into action.

Fortune had smiled upon her when she had acquired the antique dolls, so why should it not do so again? In a burst of optimism, she aimed high, and when she had acquired the missing addresses from Max and taken the packets of wedding photographs to the estate office for Huw to frank them and have them posted, another, similar packet rested unobtrusively among them.

It was addressed to one of the most exclusive fashion houses in the capital, and contained half a dozen of her most recent design ideas which, because of Max, she had not had the opportunity yet to translate into real garments.

In denying her an outlet at the local store, he had probably done her a good turn, she thought with satisfaction, and prayed that her random shot would find its mark.

However, when she left Max, she would need a roof over her head, and accommodation in the capital did not come cheap. The money for the sale of the antique dolls was crucial to her; they should fetch enough to keep her going for a considerable time. When she jumped out of the frying pan, Jess thought wryly, she would need to spread a stout net underneath beforehand, if she was not to be destroyed in the fire.

The knowledge that her designs were safely in the post, however, raised her spirits, and she hugged her secret to herself and sang softly under her breath as she went to the stables the next morning, suitably attired for her driving lesson with the sulky in her chocolate-brown jodhpurs, and a yellow sweater knitted in a fine rib that hugged the softly rounded curves of her figure underneath the gay silk cravat she knotted across the crew neckline.

Max was in the stable yard with Cloud when she got there, and to her surprise Jess saw that the stallion was saddled for riding.

'Come with me,' he suggested unexpectedly, and Jess shot him a wary look. Nina, for once, was nowhere to be seen.

Would he have invited her, Jess, to join him, if Nina had been available? she wondered cynically, and retorted, 'Bob's expecting me for a driving lesson.'

Max frowned. 'Bob's occupied with a delivery of feed that's just arrived, so you'll have to make do with your husband instead.'

'In that case, I'll go and visit the foal, and wait until he's free.' Nettled by his sarcasm, Jess turned away towards the foaling pen, but Max snubbed her to a halt.

'The mare and foal were turned out into the paddock this morning. There won't be another foal due for about ten days. You can visit that one when it arrives.'

It would not be the same. If her plans materialised for the dolls, and for the dress designs which she had sent to London, there would not be the time to get to know another foal as she had this one.

If they did not . . .

The prospect was unthinkable. Jess fought against the black depression that it threatened, and could not think of another excuse quickly enough when Max decided for her. 'I'll saddle up for you. I'll put Cloud back in his stall until I've finished.'

Jess remained beside the stallion, stroking the long nose as Cloud stuck his head over the half-doorway, plainly puzzled as to why he should be stabled again when he was kitted up for going out.

She felt a sudden affinity with the stallion's loneliness. The two stalls on either side of the one in which he was kept were empty. She assumed the occupants must be among the horses that had been turned out into the paddocks during the spell of fine weather, but, for whatever reason, it left the stallion isolated, which was how she felt herself, at bay and with no one she could turn to.

She watched as Max led her own mount across the yard, and anger rose in her as she saw that he had saddled the taller of the two horses.

If he hoped she would show signs of fear, he had mistaken her, Jess thought hardly. She would show him that she would not be browbeaten. During the course of her driving lessons, she had come to know both the horses and was used to handling them, and, although this would be her first time actually in the saddle, her initial nervousness had abated.

'Turn round and I'll give you a leg up,' Max instructed.

In the middle of the modern stable block, no other means of mounting presented itself. The animal's back was practically on a level with her own head, and Jess had no recourse but to obey him.

The contrast with her own early efforts at riding struck her forcibly as Max lifted her high.

'What's funny?' he wanted to know as her lips lifted in spite of herself.

'It just seems a far cry from using an up-ended stable bucket to scramble aboard, that's all,' she answered, readily enough.

It was not quite all. An up-ended stable bucket did not laugh up into her face like this, sharing the joke between them as Max settled her feet into the stirrups and handed her the reins.

His fingers rested lightly across her own, pressing them round the leathers, while his eyes gleamed up into hers, grey pools of provocation in the morning sunshine, daring her to test their secret depths.

Jess felt her heart lurch, and her fingers tightened convulsively on the reins; in response the animal under her began to sidle sideways. Laughter flared in the grey pools, guessing the cause of her mount's restlessness and mocking her for it, but all Max said was, 'Hold her there, and I'll join you in a second.'

He released Cloud from the stable and vaulted on to his back; Jess's heart repeated its earlier gymnastics as she watched them. The stallion was tall, but Max was taller, and the two together made an impressive sight.

He sat his mount with the easy grace of a born horseman, swaying in the saddle like a dancer to counteract the stallion's movements as it curveted with a restless energy. Quick irritation rose in Jess when Max did not rein in his mount and stop the display. It was infecting the mare, making it jig uneasily under her. Did he hope that it would unseat her, or at best frighten her sufficiently so that she would beg him to let her down? With set lips she tightened the grip of her knees, uncomfortably aware of the long distance to the ground if she did take a tumble.

'Let's get these two out into the park, and take some of the spring out of their heels,' Max called. He swung the stallion out of the stable yard, and immediately the mare straightened up and followed without any command from Jess. Just as Max himself seemed to expect her, Jess, to follow wherever he led without protest.

The comparison rasped, and to assert her independence of him Jess pressed her heels into the mare's flanks and drove it up to canter a nose ahead of the stallion. She glanced across at Max as she came up to him, and he slanted her a laughing look that read the reason behind her move, and taunted her because he was the cause.

'If you want a race, you can have one when we get out into the park proper,' he challenged her, and forged up beside her to add, 'Let's visit the mare and foal first. The mare will miss her apple and the sugar lump you've been giving her if you suddenly stop visiting her every day.'

'How do you know I've been feeding her an apple and a sugar lump?'

'Because all the animals' stable feed is closely monitored and recorded.'

'Surely a little treat now and then can't harm them, even though they're thoroughbreds?'

His remark left Jess feeling uneasy. She had only visited the foal with Max once, so how did he know what she had given to the mare when she made her daily visits to the stable alone? He seemed to be clairvoyant where she was concerned. Or, her uneasiness deepened, had Max watched her on the closed-circuit television installed in the tack-room to watch the mare and foal?

Not that it mattered. She gave a mental shrug. It simply served as a warning for her to be extra careful

with anything that she did not want him to know about,
like the designs which she had posted to London.

Max could not possibly know about those, because
she had been careful to take the envelopes to Huw just
before the mail van was due to collect the estate post,
so that her own would not be left lying around the office
for anyone to see.

She had seen the small red van come and go while
Max had been engaged at the other end of the park in
roping off the show areas, so she had nothing to worry
about on that score.

Reassured, she reined in beside Max as he drew to a
halt at the paddock rail where the mare grazed with her
foal. He vaulted lightly to the ground, and Jess slipped
her feet free from the stirrups and slid from her saddle,
eager to present her offerings to her favourite.

Instead of landing free, she slid down straight into
Max's arms. He opened them wide to receive her, and
closed them round her again like a clamp the moment
her feet touched the ground. She raised her face in quick
protest as he bent his head above her.

'A treat is the spice of life,' he murmured, mocking
her earlier question, and took a treat from her lips that
was not being offered.

The sun shone, and the light breeze sang, bending the
lush grass which the mare cropped with soft, crunching
sounds that became just another dimension of the all-
pervading silence. A pulsating silence, that wrapped itself
round Jess in a void of timelessness which swallowed up
her anger, and left only Max and herself, and the feel
of his arms moulding her to him, and the pressure of
his lips on her own.

His hands stroked subtle messages along her spine,
arousing nameless longings to fill the void. His kisses
sought answers to unspoken questions, while their

pressure denied her own lips the ability to reply except in kind.

Waves of feeling shuddered through Jess, making the world recede, and leaving only the reality of sensation that burned between herself and Max like a living current of fire. Sensations which she could not name, and feelings so elemental that she did not dare to try, but which drew her with a magnetism she was unable to resist. Helplessly she felt herself begin to submerge.

A hefty push sent them both sprawling to the ground.

Caught unaware, they rolled together on to the soft turf, to the accompaniment of an indignant whicker from the mare, which looked prepared, if necessary, to butt them again as a reminder that she did not like being kept waiting for her apple, which she had espied poking from the top of Jess's jodphur pocket.

'She wants her elevenses,' Jess gurgled. 'She doesn't like being kept waiting.'

A storm of giggles rendered her helpless as she lay on her back on the young grass and laughed up into Max's face, but her laughter died as he put his hands on either side of her prone shoulders, leaned above her, and muttered, 'She isn't the only one who doesn't like being kept waiting.'

His look burned down into her face. His colour had turned to a greyish tinge underneath his tan, and her own cheeks paled to match, her eyes wide pools of apprehension as she stared back up at him.

The mare whinnied again, a shrill cry of protest that cut across the gulf of tension between them, and Max half turned away to look at the animal over his shoulder. Quick as a flash, Jess grabbed her chance and rolled away from under him.

Gaining her feet in a desperate leap she ran to the rails, tugging the apple and the sugar lump from her pocket. With shaking hands she held them out to the mare, and stretched out her fingers towards the foal, keeping her face averted from Max.

She could sense him coming up behind her, his feet making no sound across the soft turf, and she went rigid, the muscles of her back contracting against the expected feel of his grip on her shoulders. It failed to materialise, and the foal did not come to her either.

Max gave her a long, considering look, and then went to lean his arms along the top rail of the fence, a post distant from her. The foal took two steps forward towards her, and then stopped, and watched her with wary eyes.

Jess called to it, coaxingly, but it remained out of reach, and bleakness swept over her that filled her throat with aching tears, so that she could find no words to protest when Max said abruptly, 'Let's go on. I want to inspect the enclosures.'

She would rather have gone back to the house and left him to continue with the ride on his own, but unable to speak she allowed him to lift her back into the saddle, and when he gained his own she had to be content to allow the mare to follow behind him, because her misted eyes were unable to see to guide it; she blamed the mist on the foal for rejecting her advances.

When Max was satisfied that the enclosures for the Show were roped off to his satisfaction, he turned back towards the stable and, unable to endure the loaded silence between them any longer, Jess used his earlier challenge as an excuse to bring their ride to a quick end.

She kneed her horse to the front, and called over her shoulder, 'You wanted a race. I'll beat you back to the stables.'

She stretched the mare in a ground-consuming stride. The wind whipped her hair behind her and sirened in her ears, and she thrilled to the sensation of speed as they flew across the turf.

This was riding as she had never ridden before. The gait of the thoroughbred under her was strong and effortless, needing no aids to urge it along. Behind her, she could hear the stallion's hooves thundering in pursuit, not trotting now, but freed in a full gallop.

Max's shout rang out, "Ware branch!" and Jess ducked, flattening herself across the mare's neck as it carried her under the low canopy of an ancient park tree.

The ground flashed by far beneath her, but she knew no sense of fear, only a wild exhilaration that urged her on and on, at all costs to outdistance Max.

She could not win. Weeks of assessing the stallion's speed as Max raced it round the track told Jess that, if he chose to let Cloud have his head, the stallion could outpace her own mount with ease.

So why did he not do so, and triumph?

She risked a glance over her shoulder. Max was hard on her heels, and riding easily. Was he holding the stallion in, to allow her to win the race, as he had allowed Nina to win? Patronising her?

Or was he treading on her heels, taunting her with her inability to get the better of him? Pride, spiced with temper, sent her jeer winging back to him.

'What's keeping you?'

For answer, Max galloped up beside her. Jess heard him coming. The increased tempo of the stallion's hooves drummed a warning in her ears seconds before he reached and then passed her, effortlessly forging ahead.

Right across her path.

Jess gave a gasp as, a good length in front of her, Max deliberately cut across her line of gallop, forcing her to rein in and check her mount's headlong pace, and then rein in further still as, much closer than she had realised, the end buildings of the stable block loomed through a shelter belt of trees.

'You cheated,' she accused him breathlessly as they dismounted in the stable yard minutes later. 'You cut across my path and made me slow down.'

'It's a good job for you I did, otherwise you'd have hit the building full tilt at the pace you were going.' His voice cut like the whip he disdained to carry in his hand. 'You're riding a horse, not piloting a plane. You can't take off and zoom over the top when you come on an obstacle without warning.'

Max was right, and the knowledge galled her, but to salve her pride Jess hit back.

'I'd have swerved away in plenty of time. I'm not a complete novice in the saddle.'

'Then don't behave like one.'

'You're only saying that because you were afraid I might win. I could still have got away from you if you hadn't swung across my path.'

He turned on her then. Jess tried to step back away from him, but he was too quick for her, and his fingers shot out and closed like steel clamps round her arm. He jerked her towards him and gritted, 'Don't delude yourself, Jess. You couldn't get away from me then, and you know it. Just as you know you won't ever be able to get away from me, unless I choose to let you go.'

He stared down at her for a long minute that set her heart hammering in a wild pain inside her breast, and then nearly made it stop beating altogether as he added, with a soft menace that was all the more frightening because he did not bother to raise his voice, 'And I won't let you go, Jess. Not ever. So you might as well accept it.'

CHAPTER SEVEN

JESS clutched her bag in clammy hands that made betraying marks on the patent leather as Max drove her to the fête. I could do with some of the horse aromatic, she thought without humour, and shivered at the ordeal of her speech to come.

'Ladies and gentlemen...' She gabbled it desperately to herself as they travelled. By now she knew every word by heart, and, although they were mercifully few, it seemed to her stretched nerves as if they resembled a book length.

'Huw will write a speech for you,' Max had baled her out when he discovered her biting the end of her pen over a page of writing that bore more crossings out than words, but, when she collected it from him and thanked the Welshman for his efforts, he shook his head with a smile.

'I didn't write your speech. You must thank your husband for that.'

Thanks stuck in her throat. The knowledge that Max had dictated the words she must say warred inside her, and if she had dared she would have crumpled up the paper and tossed it out of the car window.

But English garden fêtes were completely outside her experience. She visualised something stiff and formal, and knew that without the missive she would be likely to dry up and shame herself, and delight Nina and Kate Vaughan. It was easier to lower her flag in private to Max than to lay her pride open to be trampled on in public by the woman she was supplanting, however unwillingly, as the fête's guest of honour.

It made her extra careful in her choice of dress. She guessed that Kate and Nina would use the occasion to try to upstage her, and she drew on her own flawless dress sense to create the opposite effect from what she suspected might be their choice.

The day was hot, but she rejected a flowered silk that suggested itself as being ideal for the occasion, and chose instead a cool, sleeveless fondant-green linen-look dress in a starkly simple style that ideally suited her lissom figure. The material had all the attraction of linen's fine weave, and the uncrushable advantage of a man-made fibre, and with it she teamed the matching hat which she had enjoyed making for Lucy, but which looked delightful on top of her own shining bob, the pert brim just wide enough to lightly shade her eyes, and lined in white to match her accessories.

The effect was simple and stunning, and further enhanced by the uncluttered appearance of wearing no jewellery, but, even though she knew she looked good, Jess still felt apprehensive as she went downstairs to join Max.

'Will I do?' she wanted to know as she walked out to join him at the waiting Jaguar.

He turned as she approached. One hand held open the car door, and Jess felt her nerves contract as his eyes swept slowly over her, taking in every tiny detail of her appearance.

Was he comparing her to Nina and Kate Vaughan, to her own disadvantage? Her lips compressed, and then relaxed in a surge of relief that she despised herself for feeling when he drawled, 'You'll do fine. What about me?'

'You'll do fine,' she mimicked, and felt better as they laughed together, and she got into the car beside him.

Max was dressed in a lightweight suit of pale grey with a white silk shirt, and a formal blue silk tie, the perfect foil for her own cool green and white, and she knew they made a handsome couple as they parked the car and strolled together across the vicarage lawn to join the incumbent and his wife.

With masterly timing Max got them there just a couple of minutes before the opening ceremony was due to begin, long enough for them to reply to brief greetings, but not too long to wait before Jess had to begin the dreaded speech.

In spite of Sally's whispered, 'You look absolutely stunning,' she felt her throat go dry as she faced her audience.

Every VIP in the county seemed to her to be congregated in the small, roped-off area facing the dais. Kate Vaughan and Nina sat in the middle of the front row of chairs, and they both stared at Jess fixedly, with the malicious intention of putting her off her stroke. Her clammy hands told her they were succeeding only too well.

As she faced the crowd, her mind went numb. The speech she had rehearsed until she thought she was word perfect vanished like a summer snowball, and from a long way off she heard the vicar begin his introduction.

He faded into silence, and the audience clapped politely. It was her turn now to speak. Jess took no comfort from the fact that Max was standing by her side. It was his fault that she was here in the first place. His fault that the vicar was able to announce for the first time in years, 'Ladies and gentlemen, Lady Blythe,' and she hated Max for it as she forced a strained smile to her face as the clapping faded into silence, and her audience waited for her to begin.

'Ladies and gentlemen...'

Her tongue stuck. The good weather had induced a large attendance at the fête, and the sea of faces, stretched out across the lawns in front of her, seemed to Jess to go on for ever, all of them watching her, waiting for her to make the slightest slip.

Nervously she smoothed out the piece of paper in her hand and gave it a covert glance, and saw to her dismay that the words had been almost obliterated by the creases made by her nervous fingering during the journey.

She swallowed and started again, 'Ladies and gentlemen...'

Max stirred restlessly beside her, and the awful, waiting silence hung on the words that her frantic mind was totally unable to recall.

A loud buzzing sounded in her ears, and her eyes instinctively turned towards its cause, and fixed on a large striped bumble bee attracted by the flowers that crowded the brim of Kate Vaughan's hat. The milliner's decorations were overlarge and overbright, matching the florid pattern of the wearer's dress, and, unable to find the nectar it expected from them, the humming of the bee rose to an angry, frustrated buzz.

Kate heard it and, fearing aerial attack, she flapped frantically; the sudden movement unseated her handbag from her lap. It dropped to the ground and spilled its contents untidily on to the lawn, and red-faced she bent to scoop up the clutter, ignoring her daughter's audibly hissed, 'Leave them, Mother...'

Bending down nearly unseated the top-heavy hat, and Kate grabbed at it with one hand to prevent it from following the handbag. Defeated, the bee flew off to more profitable flowers.

Jess watched it go, convulsed with silent laughter. Bless the bee. Her amusement swept away her nerves, and widened her smile at her audience.

They smiled back at her, friendly faces, welcoming faces, inviting her to share their afternoon of fun. Not the stiff, formal occasion which she had dreaded, but relaxed and easy, like the gatherings she was used to in New Zealand. It made her feel easy, too, and at home among them.

Impulsively she crumpled the written speech in her hand. She no longer needed a prompt. She looked cool and poised and elegant as instead she used words that came with surprising ease to her suddenly fluent tongue.

'...This is my very first English garden fête. I do hope it will be a success. You must have all worked so hard.'

'So have you. Your dolls are smashing,' a hearty country voice called out.

Jess chuckled and called back, 'If you like them so much, then buy lots of raffle tickets. It's all in a good cause.'

Her listeners joined in the ensuing laughter and the ice was broken, and Jess did not need Max's quiet aside, 'Keep it up. You're doing fine,' to tell her that her audience was with her.

She cut the tape and declared the fête open to enthusiastic applause, and Sally said delightedly, 'They love you,' and captured her arm to lead her away among the stalls, leaving Kate Vaughan and Nina free passage to claim Max's attention.

Behind her, Jess heard Kate's over-refined voice declaring, 'So nice to see you, Max, dear,' and the euphoria faded.

She hung back and declared, 'I don't want to be liked because I'm Lady Blythe.'

Sally cast a comprehensive glance behind her and took in the scene. 'Don't be silly,' she scolded. 'They like you because you're you. You're so natural, and you don't put on any airs. And although I say it as shouldn't——' she cast a second, wary glance in the direction of her dog-collared husband '—folks do get tired of being patronised. Let's have a go at this coconut shy.'

'You're a rotten shot.' A grey-clad arm came out and removed the third ball from Jess's fingers before it could follow her other two wildly misaimed throws, and she spun round, startled, to find Max behind her, and on his own.

'Where's N...?' Her eyes stopped her tongue as she espied Nina and Kate reluctantly dragged into conversation with two elderly VIPs who preferred the shade of the marquee to the heat of the open lawn. Her eyes twinkled, and she cheered dutifully as Max let the ball fly, and hit a coconut amidships.

They gave the prize to a small boy, who ran off delightedly to show it to his mother, and earned her smiling thanks. 'There's kind...'

They bought strips of tickets at the raffle stall, and handed them back promptly to Sally to, 'give them to somebody. You'll know best who.'

Jess felt a silly pride when Max said admiringly, 'Your dolls look super.'

She had managed in the end to dress two for the fête, and they took pride of place on the stall. Sally had marked them as first and second prizes in the main raffle, and Kate Vaughan's offering of a box of toiletries which, Jess surmised from its slightly worn look, was probably an unwanted present from last Christmas, was the third prize, another cause for discontent for the owner of the over-decorated hat. Jess felt more than ever glad that she had followed her instinct and dressed with her usual classic simplicity.

As they strolled together, invitations to join various village activities were showered upon her from every side, all of them offered with a genuine warmth that she could not doubt were for her company alone, and not because

she came from the castle. How could she explain that
she did not intend to remain there for long enough to
be able to join in anything?

The answer was that she could not, and so she smiled
and murmured non-committal replies that drew from
Max a curt, 'You're not obliged to make a hermit of
yourself. There's a good social life going on in the village.
If you don't join in, you'll never make friends.'

Friendship was a long-term commitment and, although
Jess felt as if she needed friends as never before, they
were a luxury she could not indulge while she remained
at the castle, because the more things, or people, she
became involved with, the more difficult it would be
eventually to extricate herself when she left.

She was aware of Max's searching glance, like a radar
beam striving to read her thoughts, and hastily she
switched them off, and turned away to try her luck at
the tombola.

They visited all the stalls in turn. Max spent freely,
and following his lead Jess did the same. Several times
Nina and Kate tried to thrust their way through the crowd
to join them. Was it pure coincidence, Jess wondered,
that each time Sally managed to waylay them, and they
ended up talking to somebody else, while she and Max
made the rounds together unhindered?

It was too much to hope that her luck would continue,
however, and Jess steeled herself on their way out as the
pair caught up with them in the paddock that had been
turned into a car park for the day.

'Thank goodness that's another ghastly event over,'
Kate declared with an exaggerated sigh. Her face looked
as if her feet hurt, and she used her overburdened hat
to fan herself with.

Max gave her a surprised look. 'You always said you
enjoyed these dos.'

'Oh, I make the effort, for the sake of the locals. But it's not really in our line, is it?' She included Max, but not Jess, in her snobbish assumption. 'The stalls are full of home-made stuff. All very worthy, but you can buy better in town.'

So much for my dolls, thought Jess, and drew reassurance from the venom in the older woman's voice that must be a measure of her own success, as Kate went on, 'For people who prefer sophisticated entertainment, these village dos have got to be the ultimate in boredom.' The look she cast towards the armful of oddments which Jess had collected during her round of the stalls was eloquent, and it stung Jess into retaliation.

'In that case I must be very unsophisticated, because I thoroughly enjoyed myself,' she put in sweetly, and realised to her surprise that she was telling no more than the truth.

This was no time to stop and examine her discovery, however, and she hurried on before Kate could speak again. 'Will you open the car door for me, please, Max, so that I can put these on the seat before I drop them?'

To her relief Max complied straight away, and she hid a grin as he took her parcels from her arms one by one, and laid them carefully along the back seat for her, presenting a rear view himself to the two Vaughan women that even they must find difficulty in communicating with.

Balked, they turned away to their own car drawn up nearby, but not before Nina had one more try.

'I'll see you at the dance.' She ignored Jess and addressed Max, but she had not chosen her moment well. He was carefully fitting a pot of home-made jam in between a sticky-looking cream sponge and some home-made scones.

He did not turn round, but called instead over his shoulder, 'We'll be there.'

'Do come and open the car door for me, Nina, there's a dear. I must sit down,' Kate Vaughan called plaintively, capitulating to the torment of her spiky-heeled shoes. With a venomous look at Jess, Nina had no option but to go to her mother's rescue, and before she could return Max had shut the back door of the Jaguar, and joined Jess in the front seat.

They both waved to the Vaughans as they drove away, but they were out of the paddock gate and away along the lane, and did not see whether the two waved back. Jess did not care as Max said casually, 'Did you really mean that?'

'Mean what?' Now they were back in the car together, and without the distraction of the crowd around them, Jess's tension returned.

'That you enjoyed yourself.'

'Yes, why not? Once I got over the speech bit, the rest was fun. It wasn't a bit like I expected.'

'What did you expect?'

'A boiled-shirt sort of gathering, I suppose. All terribly English and stuck up and formal. But instead everyone was relaxed and friendly, quite different from what I imagined they'd be.'

'If you'd give your imagination a rest, you might find reality more acceptable in a lot of things, not just garden fêtes.'

Hinting that it was her own fault that she did not find the reality of her position as his wife acceptable? Jess stiffened, and changed the subject.

'Cook might not find it acceptable if I bring back a lot of foodstuff from the fête that other people have made. She might regard it as a slight on her own efforts.'

'We'll take it all down to the stables. The young lads there will make short work of the cake and the jam for you. I've got some post to take to the estate office for

Huw to send out on Monday, so we might as well go there first before we go back to the house.'

Max distributed the goodies to the stable lads with the stern warning, 'Don't stuff Cloud with any of this,' and laughed at the chorused assurance, 'He hasn't got a chance,' as the lads settled down on a straw bale to enjoy the unexpected booty.

Jess was still smiling at the success of her gift as she followed Max into the estate office. It being a Saturday, Huw was not on duty, and Max said, 'I'll leave my post in the "out" tray, and book it into the post book ready for Monday morning.'

The post book? Jess frowned as he opened a desk drawer and drew out a thick, ledger-like volume, and laid it open at a half written-up page, which she saw with dismay was drawn up into columns of what looked like dates, addresses, and cost of postage.

She held her breath as Max began to write. When she brought the packets of wedding photographs, and her own one, precious envelope of designs addressed to the fashion house in London, had Huw entered the addresses in the post book?

If so, would Max's sharp eye pick out the one now from the rest of the post she had brought to the estate office that day? Perhaps there was enough post going through the office daily to fill a double page, in which case her own packet might not be on the opened leaves at all.

Now the door to her freedom was opening to her, secrecy was paramount, and the fear that Max might somehow discover what she had done, and once more find a way to thwart her, perhaps even to intercept an answer to her letter, if there was one, made Jess's nerves scream with tension.

She craned forward to try to read the writing, and Max glanced up at her, alerted by her movement, which she explained hurriedly with, 'I was just admiring the writing. It's almost copperplate.'

Max's own firm script was above criticism, but he agreed readily enough. 'It's good, isn't it? Huw does it. He writes the place cards if we have any functions at the Castle, and it makes a dinner-table look special.'

Jess was not interested in the writing, only in the identity of the writer who had dealt with her own package, but she was not close enough to be able to make out the individual addresses. If she tried, she might arouse Max's curiosity, and make him read through them even if he had not done so before, so perforce she had to remain unsatisfied when he closed the book and put it away.

'Let's have a look at the mare before we go back and get changed for the dance,' he said.

Bob had already installed a new mother-to-be in the foaling box, and Max studied her carefully on the television screen in the tack-room before they left and drove back to the house.

The dance to follow the fête was being held in the village hall and, as it was a barn dance, they did not need to dress up.

'Open-necked shirt for me, and something pretty for you,' Max said thankfully, and true to his word he appeared soon afterwards looking coolly elegant in midnight blue trousers and a lighter blue, short-sleeved shirt, open at the neck to reveal the darkly tanned column of his throat.

The sight of it sent a strange feeling shafting through Jess, possessing her fingers with an errant longing to stroke the long, strong pillar that supported his head, and she clenched her hands into the pocket of her brightly patterned dirndl skirt in an effort to subdue such unwanted urges.

Backing her judgement for the second time, she wore the exact opposite in style for the dance from the clothes she had had on during the afternoon. The vivid colours of her full cotton skirt ranged from dark, burnt orange, to palest primrose, with a yellow top to match, and her gay outfit infected her mood.

Her guess that Nina would try to copy what she had worn at the fête, by putting on something plain, was proved correct. The other girl's cocktail dress was a shocking-pink silk, beautifully cut, and, Jess guessed shrewdly, very expensive. It was ideal for a smart social function, but it was wildly out of place at a barn dance.

Nina's expression of rage as she caught sight of Jess's bright outfit said clearly enough that she knew she had come off second best once again, and she joined the line of dancers with a flounce that boded ill for the comfort of her partner.

The caller captured Jess's attention as he began to chant, 'Take your partners,' and soon she became lost in the catchy music, and the exuberant measure of the dance.

The steps carried her along to other partners, and then back again to Max, and it did the same to Nina, but it gave Jess some satisfaction that for once the other girl was unable to monopolise Max, and was obliged to dance and pass on, the same as all the rest.

Nina's partner appeared to be a strong-minded individual, because when the interval came he foiled her bid to break away from him and go to Max, and held on to her firmly, steering her to the opposite end of the room. Max did not appear to notice the minor fracas, but collected a cool drink for himself and Jess from the buffet, and took her to be introduced to the local cricket team.

'Max is our star bowler,' the captain, a burly young farmer, told her as he shook her heartily by the hand.

Max laughed and quipped, 'That isn't what he tells me when we're playing.'

'Come and join us at the next match, and judge for yourself, Lady Blythe,' chimed in another member of the team.

'Call me Jess.'

She was making it harder for herself every minute, Jess thought despairingly, but her own friendly nature could not help but respond to the warmth that greeted her from every side. Her eyes still sparkled with the zest of the dance and the merry company, and she laughed and raised her glass along with the others as they proposed a toast to the success of the next cricket match.

And when the band drew them all back again on to the floor, in sets of eight, with the others still around to act as a buffer between herself and Max, Jess threw caution to the winds, laid aside her defences, and rode on the crest of the music and the moment, relying on it to keep her thoughts at bay while she gave herself up to enjoying the rest of the evening.

The caller abruptly removed her buffer, and uncovered her mistake, when unexpectedly he announced that, by special request, the last dance would be a waltz, and Max immediately claimed it as his. Had he been the one to make the special request?

They had not danced together like this since their wedding night, and now everything was subtly different. Then, Max had been host at the castle ball, as well as bridegroom, dressed in formal clothes, and cloaked in formal behaviour.

Now, freed from such constraints and in casual dress, he seemed to Jess's heightened sensitivity to be less threatening, and closer, but infinitely more dangerous.

The defences which she had thrust aside so recklessly only moments before left her wide open and vulnerable to the smouldering virility that radiated from Max like a living fire. It melted her spine where his hands came into contact with her back, and paralysed the power of her mind to resist the vibes that flowed from him like invisible radar beams, searching for, and finding, a response.

Dismayed, she felt her senses leap to meet them, clamouring like winged creatures to be set free from a cage, and as the lights dimmed round them, marooning each dancing couple in their own secret, private world of darkness, Max bent his head, and unlocked the door with his lips.

Helpless to prevent herself, Jess felt her body go pliant in his arms, and a tremor passed through her as she raised wide eyes to his face. Her heart pounded with slow, suffocating beats, every other one performing the by now familiar crazy somersault in her breast that made it difficult for her to breath, and her limbs moved automatically, mesmerised by the music and the movement—and Max.

His lips stroked hers. 'Happy?' he murmured, and, immobilised under the pressure of his lips, Jess's own lips were capable only of a muffled reply.

'Mmmm.'

They lied. How could he expect her to be happy, under the circumstances? Or did his question merely embrace this evening, this moment, and carefully leave aside all the other questions to which her increasingly bewildered mind strove without success to supply an answer?

Soft though her murmur was, his ears caught it, and his mouth curved in a smile against her own, stretching her lips in a mirror smile which they performed with a curious ease.

To Jess's consternation, her mumbled reply did hold an element of truth, in spite of her wish to deny it. It, too, ignored the wider issues, and concentrated only on the magic of gliding in Max's arms through the soft darkness, drawn close by the silver thread of music.

The thread snapped abruptly as the lights went up. The tempo of the dance quickened, and a few circuits of the room later it came to an end, and goodnights began to echo round the hall.

Jess went with the others to collect her coat from the cloakroom. Nina was there, battling as usual to be first among the crush of people, and momentarily the eddy of departing dancers thrust them together. Nina hissed in her ear, 'You've won, *this time*,' before she grabbed her own coat and thrust her way outside to her partner.

Jess ignored her. She had something more important than Nina's spite to occupy her mind at the moment. Her brain spun. During the last waltz, Max had succeeded in getting through to her as he had not done before, and the chaotic state of her feelings was a pointer to just how effective his methods had been.

She was silent on the way home, grateful that Max had used the Range Rover in order to give a lift to several of the younger members of the castle staff who wanted to attend the dance.

Their tireless chatter saved her from the burden of conversation during the journey, but once indoors her respite was short-lived as the housekeeper appeared with a tray of coffee and biscuits, and foiled her attempt to escape immediately upstairs. Reluctantly she followed Max into the drawing-room while Mrs Kirk ushered the young staff members off to their own quarters. The room door shut behind the housekeeper, leaving Jess and Max alone.

Silence wrapped round them when she was gone. An endless, pregnant silence, through which Jess's nerve-tuned ears caught the sound of a hunting owl calling across the darkness of the park, and other small night sounds, of which she was aware only as a vague background.

And then she was aware only of Max as he caught her to him and their lips fused, and she did not know whether her riotous pulse registered elation or despair as Max set about cutting the last lifeline by which she held on to her wavering self-control. She felt herself slowly begin to slip beneath the overpowering waves of kisses, which he rained ceaselessly upon her face.

The extension telephone, sitting on the occasional table beside them, shocked her back to the surface. Its summons was loud and shrill and refused to be silenced, and with a muttered oath Max dropped his arms from round her, and reached out for the receiver.

Who could be ringing them at this time of night? Jess wondered. Surely not Nina? She felt a burning resentment that it might be Nina who had disturbed them.

The man's voice answering Max's curt, 'Yes?' was unmistakably that of Bob Tempest. Equally unmistakably, he was a very worried man.

Max held the receiver between them, away from his ear, tacitly sharing the call with Jess, and the message came through to her quite clearly.

'The mare in the foaling-box has gone down, Max. She's in deep trouble. There was no warning. She just folded. I've sent for the vet, but I think you should come, if you possibly can.'

'I'm on my way.'

For a long moment Max stood looking down at Jess, his eyes devouring the delicate outline of her face tipped up to his like a pale flower in the soft lamplight. He towered above the standard lamp, which was the only illumination they had bothered to switch on, and it left his face in shadow, so that Jess was unable to read its expression.

Her every nerve-end was finely tuned to a vivid awareness of him, waiting for him to speak, wanting him to stay silent. Not knowing what...or who...she wanted.

She jinked away from answering her own question, and the owl hooted again. It was like a signal. An omen. Suddenly Jess shivered, and slight though the movement was it broke the spell between them.

Max put down the receiver with a decisive click, like a knife cutting across their closeness, cutting her apart from him and leaving her stranded.

Impulsively, Jess laid her hand on his sleeve and begged, 'Let me come with you,' but he put her aside and refused.

'No, I may be up all night. You'd best go to bed.'

If Bob had not called, would he have joined her there tonight? Jess felt shaken by a sudden, wild longing for him to join her, and by sick disappointment that he was going to attend to the mare instead.

What had come over her? she wondered, aghast. Bob Tempest had just given her the narrowest escape she'd had yet, not only from Max, she acknowledged honestly, but from herself as well, and she ought to be blessing the stable manager for his intervention, instead of wishing that the telephone system was out of order.

Cold with dismay, she heard the front door shut behind Max as he hurried away, and then the Range Rover engine purred into life, and she strained her ears to catch the last faint sound until it finally disappeared into silence, and the night.

She turned then, and made her slow way upstairs. She undressed and climbed into bed, where she lay wide-eyed and wakeful, counting the regular signals from the grandfather clock in the hall downstairs that told the passing hours, but Max did not return.

He came back at breakfast time, but only briefly to eat, shave and shower, before he returned to the stables.

'The mare will need round-the-clock attention if we're to save the foal,' he answered Jess's anxious question. 'Bob and I are going to take it in turns to stay with her, for as long as it takes.'

It took several days, during which time Jess saw him only at brief intervals. No one was allowed in the foaling-box except Max, Bob and the vet. Nina tried to gain access, and was curtly ordered out by the vet, and she took her ban with sulky ill grace which did not help the already brittle atmosphere existing between her and Jess.

Jess continued to drive the sulky each day, albeit without Bob's guidance, and in a bid to help out the stable staff, who were stretched by their manager having to give his sole attention to the mare, she also rode daily, helping to exercise the mares stabled, like Cloud, but at the far end of the stable complex, some distance from the stallion.

Nina rode into the yard one morning just as Jess was saddling up, ready to take a mare out. She had already had her session with the sulky, careful to use the track before Nina could arrive and claim it.

Jess did not particularly want a confrontation with the other girl while Max was absorbed in trying to save the mare and the foal, since Nina would doubtless use an argument as an excuse to demand that Max should leave his work and come and referee, and Jess guessed shrewdly that the blame for dragging him away from the mare would fall upon her own head, and play right into Nina's hands.

For this reason she did not insist that Nina remove her mount which, when she returned from her ride, she discovered the other girl had stabled in the loose-box which belonged to the mare she had just exercised.

Nina must have known this, since she had seen the horse being led out, and Jess accused her sharply, 'You did that on purpose. Why didn't you turn your horse into the paddock, the same as you always do when you ride over here?'

Nina was hoping to make trouble, Jess saw vexedly, and she was determined to thwart her, so when the other girl shrugged, 'Why the fuss? There are a couple of empty boxes on either side of Cloud,' Jess swallowed her anger, and, slipping off her mare's saddle, she opened the door of the loose-box next to the stallion, and turned the mare inside ready for the stable lad to groom her.

Cloud was missing Max, and she had made a habit of fondling the grey as she passed his box each morning. She turned to do so now, but instead of the soft whicker she expected, and the gentle nuzzling of the big head, Cloud tossed her hands roughly aside, and let out a shrill call that trumpeted across the stable yard.

The mare Jess had just stabled in the next-door loose-box answered the call, and the sound appeared to drive the stallion mad. Its nostrils flared and its eyes grew wild; Jess recoiled in horror as it lunged at the stable door, striving to jump free. Finding its way blocked, it lashed out at the stout wooden barrier, splintering the planks under its lunging hooves.

In seconds, pandemonium reigned.

Men came running from all directions: Max, Bob and the stable lads. Max called out a sharp order, and two boys raced into the box where Jess had put the mare, and emerged with the animal prancing between them. Their hands held tight on either side of the head leathers, they raced the mare away between them towards the far end of the stable complex, and the loose-box that Nina had usurped.

The sight of the mare retreating excited the stallion to still greater efforts to get free, but the door held, and he worked out his frustration by commencing to demolish his loose-box with his hooves, accompanying the destruction with fearsome screams of rage that made Jess's blood run cold.

It froze into ice as she saw Max reach out to open the stable door and go inside.

'Max, no!' she screamed. 'You'll be killed.'

Her paralysed limbs unlocked, and she ran towards him and grasped hold of his sleeve.

'If I am, what do you care?' His face was contorted, his eyes as wild and furious as those of his stallion, turned from grey to black with a rage that made the destructive force inside the stable pale by comparison. 'Get out,' he snarled, and thrust her roughly away from him. 'Get out, while you're still safe.'

Safe from the stallion, or safe from himself? His searing look answered her unspoken question, and Jess staggered back and watched appalled, as Max flung back the bolt, slipped inside the stable, and rammed the bolt back home behind him before the horse could leap free.

Deliberately locking himself in with those tearing teeth and flashing hooves. A cry that was a moan broke from Jess's ashen lips.

'Max...'

She *did* care. She had not known it herself until a few seconds ago. Max still did not know. Perhaps, now, he never would.

The knowledge hit Jess like a thunderbolt, and she received the blow with numb acceptance. Thunderbolts were minor things compared to the danger Max faced in the stable.

She loved her husband.

She must have loved him all along, but had not known it. When he had reached out to pull the bolt on the stable door, it was as if his hand had unbolted a storehouse of self-knowledge inside her which escaped with a rush, as the stallion could not.

It was all irrelevant now. Jess closed her eyes and
prayed.

The crashing noises seemed as if they would go on for
ever. Over them, she could hear Max speaking in a calm,
soothing tone. Gradually the crashing grew less fre-
quent, and out of a great emptiness inside her another
voice spoke. Bob's voice.

'It's all right, Jess. Max is safe. He's coming out.'

Safe, but injured. Jess pressed her fingers to her lips
to stifle her cry of dismay as Max slid out of the stable
door, cradling his one arm with the other, and told the
stable manager hoarsely, 'Bolt the door quickly, Bob.'
He leaned against it while the stable manager complied,
then added, 'Leave Cloud for an hour to calm down,
then give him a bran mash. I'll have to get my wrist
attended to.'

It was visibly swelling, and his hand dangled limp at
the end of it as if it were bereft of motive power. Jess
felt her stomach churn. His wrist must be broken, and
who knew what other damage besides, and it was her
fault.

She longed to run to him and cradle the injured arm
in her arms, and plead with him that she was sorry. Tell
him that she loved him. But the bleak dismissal of his
angry eyes forbade her, and she accepted with trembling
certainty that the only reason he allowed her to drive
him to the local hospital was because there was no one
else free who could drive the car for him. Bob and the
stable lads all had their hands full, and Nina was nowhere to be seen. The girl had disappeared as soon as
the uproar started, to where Jess neither knew nor cared.

She waited tensely while Max had his wrist X-rayed,
and a brisk young doctor read the result. 'It isn't broken,
but it's very badly sprained. There shouldn't be any per-
manent damage, but you won't be able to use it for at
least a week or ten days, in case you've torn any of the

guides. It's hard to tell while it's so swollen. I'll take another X-ray in about a week's time to make sure, and in the meantime I'll immobilise it so that you can't use it.'

'A week?' Max's expression became grimmer, if possible, than before. 'I'm due to drive in a race in three days' time.'

''Fraid not.' The doctor shook his head emphatically. 'You won't have any feeling in your fingers until it starts to heal, so driving anything will be out of the question.'

Especially driving a sulky.

A sensitive touch on the reins was essential to establish contact between horse and driver, particularly in a race. Jess offered tentative comfort with, 'Bob will take over for you. You've said yourself that he's a fine driver. He'll race Cloud.'

'Bob can't take my place,' Max snarled. 'A change of driver or horse isn't allowed at such short notice for a cup race.' He turned stormy eyes on Jess as she slid behind the wheel of the Jaguar to take him home, and he got in awkwardly beside her, spurning her offer of help. 'Thanks to you, the success I need to establish Cloud has been thrown to the winds. All the years of training have been a complete waste of time. Perhaps, now, you're satisfied.'

'*Satisfied?* What on earth are you talking about?'

'If you wanted to get your own back because I made you marry me, you couldn't have chosen a better way to do it.'

The injustice of it took Jess's breath away. It had not been her fault. The temporary weakness that had made her willing to acknowledge that it was died in the flames of her anger, and she flared, 'You can't blame me for what happened. How was I to know that Cloud would suddenly go mad like that?'

'What did you expect, when you put an in-season mare into the box next to a stallion, where he could see her, and wind her, and not get at her? Animals haven't got the same self-control as human beings,' he lashed her bitterly.

The inference was too obvious to miss, and Jess gave a gasp. 'I didn't know the mare was in season. I've never had anything to do with breeding horses.'

'Why do you imagine I keep the two loose-boxes on either side of Cloud's stable empty? I don't waste valuable space for fun.'

'Nina told me to use the box next to Cloud. She'd put her horse into my mare's stable, so I had to take the animal somewhere.'

'You're talking nonsense. Nina wouldn't do such a crazy thing. She breeds her own horses, and she knows better than to risk exciting a thoroughbred stallion.'

Nina had known, but it was useless to argue with Max in his present mood. Nina had deliberately filled the mare's loose-box with her own horse, so that Jess would be obliged to put the mare in the only other available one, next to Cloud, knowing what the outcome would be, and that Max would blame Jess. Knowing that, in the ensuing uproar, someone might be badly hurt, and, incredibly, not caring.

Jess cared, and relief that the consequences had not been even more serious for Max warred with anguish as she tried to come to terms with something that was much worse than Cloud missing the race, worse even than a loveless marriage.

A marriage where one partner loved, and the other one hated.

CHAPTER EIGHT

THE morning post brought Jess a reply from the fashion house in London.

Max had not, as she'd feared, intercepted the letter, which meant he could not have noticed Huw's entry in the post book, she thought with relief, and she slit open the envelope with a hand that trembled with excitement.

It was quite safe for her to investigate the contents, since Max was not there. In spite of his injured wrist, he had already departed for the stables.

He had answered her enquiry, 'How is it, this morning?' with a curt, 'Out of commission, of course,' and had strode out of the room, leaving Jess burning at the injustice of his blame.

Max had declined breakfast, and she had no appetite for it either. She straightened out the letter and devoured the neatly typed script inside.

Its contents were all that she had hoped for, and more. The fashion house was delighted with the designs she had sent to them, and wanted more. They wanted to use her idea of doll-sized models in the windows of their Bond Street store to launch their next spring fashion display, and would like to see her in London as soon as possible to discuss a contract between them.

The words on the page seemed to dance in front of Jess's eyes. Why had this not happened before she met Max, while she was still free, and heart whole?

Slowly she returned the letter to its envelope. The door to freedom, which she had fought so hard to open, had now been flung wide for her, but contrarily she no longer wanted to step through, and knew that she must, because to remain at Blythe only invited further heartache. The torment of remaining with Max, of loving him and all the time knowing that her love was not returned, would be unendurable.

There was no time for her to reply to the letter now. The County Show opened that afternoon, and she had to perform the ceremony. The cheerful bustle, the bunting and the bright sunshine that would draw the crowds in flocks, were a hollow mockery to Jess as she made her way to the estate office with the rest of the post.

It comprised the usual crop of invitations to open various functions which she would not be around long enough to attend, and she wrote 'no' across each one. The only thing she would open from now on would be a tin.

Huw was not in his office, and she ran him to earth in the stable yard, talking to Max. Nina was there as well. Jess hesitated, and then forced herself forward.

No matter what Max chose to believe, the episode of the day before was not her fault, and she refused to feel guilty about it and act as if it was.

The vet came out of the stallion's stable as Jess walked up to the small group, and she eyed him apprehensively. Had Cloud injured himself, after all? Her stomach tied itself in a tight knot. Max would hate her if the stallion had damaged itself in any way when it was trying to crash free from its stable.

No one spoke. The tension was electric as the vet came up, and the relief was like an audible ripple among them as he pronounced, 'Cloud's fine, Max. Not a scratch or a bruise on him. He'll get over his tantrum. We all have to, don't we?'

He grinned, and then sobered as Huw put in, 'I was going to ask you about the foal, Max.'

'The mare aborted.' Max turned accusing eyes on Jess, and added, 'It was inevitable, after the uproar here yesterday.'

The tension returned fourfold. Huw looked desperately uncomfortable. Max's face was tight and unforgiving, and Jess flushed and then went pale. Miserably she wished she had not come. Nina looked smug. The eyes of the elderly vet went from one revealing face to another, and he broke in with a bluff, 'Can't be helped. These things happen. I'll do the post-mortem and let you know the results as soon as I can, Max. More to the point, how's your wrist?'

'Out of action for at least a week. Which means I can't race Cloud for the cup,' Max ground out savagely.

The vet gave a grimace of sympathy. 'That's real hard luck, to be put out of the cup race by an accident at the last minute. A win would have put Cloud on the map.'

'It's harder luck still when the accident happens to be your own wife,' Nina said sweetly, and her tinkling laugh grated on Jess's ears as the other girl turned to her and enquired, 'How does it feel to score an own goal?'

Jess could not have answered the question, even if she had wanted to. The chaotic state of her own feelings defied analysis. The most recognisable among the simmering cauldron was anger—against Max, against Nina. Temporarily, it eclipsed even her love for Max. The depths of her anger shocked Jess, and hardened into a rock-like determination.

Nina should not get away with this.

From the very beginning, she had set out to make trouble. Then it had not mattered, because Jess did not care, but now she did, and she vowed to teach Nina a lesson if it was the last thing she did.

It probably *would* be the last thing she did while she was at Blythe, and the knowledge lay like a grey pall over her spirits, but determinedly she squared her

shoulders and, ignoring the other girl, she dropped her
letters on Huw's lap. With a nod to the vet, she walked
away, and saw with satisfaction that her move had the
effect of breaking up the group.

The vet took Max's arm and strolled towards the
foaling pen, from which everyone else was still barred,
including Nina.

Huw sent his electric wheelchair whirring back towards
the estate office, and Nina was left standing on her own.
She stood nonplussed, tapping the top of her riding boot
with her cane until, realising that no one was inviting
her to go with them, she stalked off towards the Show
ground, doubtless to give the organiser a hard time, Jess
surmised.

She herself went in search of the head stable lad. She
knew she was a favourite among the stable staff; her
own natural friendliness during her daily visits there ensured their liking, and her offering of cakes from the
garden fête had firmly cemented their goodwill.

She ran her quarry to earth grooming the mare that
had been the cause of all the trouble yesterday. The
young face was serious as the lad went about his task,
whistling between his teeth as he brushed. The news
about the foal, and Cloud's lost race, had spread gloom
among the stables.

His expression lightened into incredulity as, perching
herself on a straw bale, Jess poured her brainwave into
his receptive ears.

'D'you think you can?' he burst out as she finished.
'I mean, are you up to it? Cloud's strong. He takes a
bit of holding.'

'I can only try. If anything goes wrong, I'll take full
responsibility. You won't be implicated. But I need your
help. I can't do it by myself. I'll be tied up Lady Blythe-
ing with the VIPs until the last moment, and there won't

be time for me to do anything else but slip away and get changed.'

'You can count on me.' The stable lad's eyes shone with excitement, plentifully mixed with admiration.

Jess smiled and replied, 'I do,' and went away well satisfied that she had an ally who could be relied upon to keep her secret to himself.

Buoyed up by the knowledge, she performed the opening ceremony that afternoon with an aplomb that astonished her, although she was careful this time to stick to the words of the speech which Huw had written out for her.

The subsequent entertaining during the evenings at the castle, in which she and Max would be involved until the Show was over, Jess welcomed as a buffer to see her through the days until she could take up the offer in the letter from the fashion house, and make her escape to London.

She planned to take the antique dolls with her. In odd moments she managed to finish redressing them, and the replica clothes were authentic in both pattern and appearance. She was well pleased with the result, and her earlier researches suggested several avenues of sale that would welcome the dolls, and give her a fair price for them—enough, with luck, to fund her freedom.

The ache in the region of her heart denied that she would ever be free from Max, but sternly she thrust its plaint aside. First, she had to complete the task which she had set herself at the castle.

The three days of the Show were a wearing round of socialising, in which she and Max were always together, and never alone. Their presence was demanded on all sides.

As well as opening the Show, Jess found herself drawn into presenting cups and rosettes, patting the noses of prize cattle, shaking winning show jumpers by the hand,

and admiring exhibits of agricultural machinery, the use of which remained a complete mystery to her.

They paused beside Sally's craft tent, to be told gleefully, 'All those dolls you gave us were sold first off. We've made a huge amount of money for the minibus,' and then passed on to congratulate proud mothers at the bonny baby competition.

Instinctively Jess reached out and picked up the winner, and the lively nine-month-old crowed and kicked. The small warm bundle in her arms sent a shaft of pain through Jess that made her gasp at its intensity.

Delighted with the attention bestowed upon her baby, the young mother beamed, and meeting her eyes, Jess felt as if her own must have turned as green as the turf on which she stood, with envy for the other woman's happiness. Who knew, the plump and smiling mother might have envied Lady Blythe her model figure, her designer clothes, or her title. She could not know how Jess envied her the baby, the child of a love that could not be bought.

She, Jess, would willingly trade every benefit that her future career might bestow upon her in order to receive such love from Max, but it was not to be. She was the substitute bride, and now the substitute wife, replacing Lucy in his home, but not in his heart.

She could feel Max's eyes fixed on her face, probing every slight change of expression, and lest he should read too much Jess hurriedly handed the baby back to its mother and passed on to look at yet more farm machinery, which was cold and impersonal and hurt less.

The harness racing was to be the final big event of the last day, and it drew huge crowds to watch the contest. The racing fraternity from several countries was present, and Jess knew with a sinking heart that they had all come with one thing in mind, the determination to win the prestigious cup that would put their own horse on the map for both racing and breeding.

The prestige which Max coveted for Cloud, and which, without having the stallion to compete against, Nina's horse stood an excellent chance of winning.

In spite of his self-control, Max was unable to prevent the bleakness from showing in his eyes as he watched the forgathering of the contestants, of which, but for his injured wrist, he would have been one. The commiseration of his guests as he led them to the enclosure allotted to the VIPs among the serried ranks of seats merely added salt to the wound.

Jess whispered, 'Before the racing starts, I must get out of these high-heeled shoes. They're killing me. I'll nip back and change, and join you again in a few minutes.'

The simmering anger showed in Max's voice as he snapped back, 'What did you put them on for in the first place? You've worn comfortable slip-ons until now.'

She had deliberately worn high heels today so that, if all else failed, she would have a valid excuse to return to the house before the harness racing started, and before Max could do anything to prevent her she sent a smiling, 'Back in a moment,' towards the guests, and hurried away.

Back in a moment, but not to the VIP stand.

Pushing time, Jess fled to the stable yard, and the tackroom where she had earlier secreted her riding kit. It took only seconds to fling aside the elegant hat and dress, and the high-heeled shoes, and don riding boots and jodphurs, and the silk shirt that bore the racing stripes of green and gold which proclaimed them as belonging to Blythe.

The garment was made to fit Max, and it drowned Jess, but by judicious use of safety pins she made sure it would not drop off her half-way round the track, and blessed the head lad for his co-operation when she settled herself on to the sulky seat, and ordered the ready-harnessed Cloud to, 'Walk on.'

Cautiously she had rubbed horse aromatic generously on to her forehead and hands, but it was not really necessary. An icy calm invaded her. She replied to the head lad's anxious, 'Are you sure you can manage, Lady Blythe? Cloud's in a frisky mood,' with a cool, 'Quite sure. Don't worry,' and tacked herself on to the end of the line of competitors to name herself to the steward as they passed on to the track.

She could not be more sure, and it was too late to worry. The steward, armed with his clipboard, was one competitor ahead, and momentarily Jess closed her eyes and prayed.

If the entry gave Max's full name, she would not be allowed to compete. If it even said, 'Mr M J Beaumont,' she would be lost. The competitor in front of her passed on, and Jess's tongue felt stiff as the man, a stranger, read out, 'M J Beaumont?'

Not Maxwell Jonathan, or Mr M J Beaumont. Just the initials, and the name, which she, too, could truthfully claim as her own.

Jess nodded, and confirmed jubilantly, 'Margaret Jess Beaumont.' She let out a long breath of relief as the man clipped her racing number on the leathers of Cloud's head, and waved her through.

The disc bore the number seven, her lucky number. It was like an omen, and her spirits lifted as Jess joined the rest of the field. Deliberately she made sure she would be the last one on to the track, to lessen the chance of Max seeing her and trying to intervene.

She drew an outside position among the second tier of runners, and hunched down on her seat to try to make herself as inconspicuous as possible. Max would not

expect to see her on the track, so there was just the chance
that he might miss her among the large field.

She had only just taken her place when a shrill protest
came from the first line of runners, as Nina looked round
and caught sight of her.

'This woman can't compete,' she shouted, and waved
the steward over with a furious signal. 'Her name isn't
the one on the race card. I protest.'

The steward hurried over and consulted his card again.
'It says here, M J Beaumont, and those are the lady's
initials. Protest overruled. Get into line, and move off
behind the starting vehicle.'

Perforce Nina had to obey, or risk being disqualified
herself for obstruction, but the contretemps attracted the
attention of the crowd, and Jess condemned the girl
fiercely under her breath as, across the sea of faces in
the stands, she felt Max's attention beam on to her.

The green and gold stripes of her shirt seemed to stand
out like a banner, pinpointing her among the other competitors, and she breathed urgently to the grey hind-
quarters in front of her, 'Don't let him stop me now.
He mustn't stop me now.'

Across the distance she could feel Max's anger
reaching out to grip her, lashing her for destroying his
own chances of competing in the race, and then for
taking his place and doing the unforgivable by risking
his precious stallion for the second time, in her own in-
experienced hands.

If they did not start off soon, he might still be able
to stop her from competing.

'Ready? Start rolling,' the steward called out, and it
was too late now for Max to interfere. She was on her
own.

The mobile starting gate moved off, and the field followed it, and with desperate concentration Jess dragged
her mind away from Max and fixed it on keeping Cloud

in line with the others as they moved with increasing speed behind the converted Land Rover.

The stallion's ears were pricked forward, eager to be off, and as the moving barrier swung clear, and the Land Rover carrying it peeled away off the track, the horses and sulkies got away at a fast clip.

Cloud was the perfect racing machine. The thrill of driving the stallion for the first time captured Jess, and swept everything else from her mind as she manoeuvred up through the field of competitors, going easily, but not too fast, because there were two more heats yet to come.

The speed as they reached the home straight had already weeded out those who stood a chance from those who did not, and it was a much depleted field that pointed the horses towards the winning post.

Nina had drawn an inside position, which gave her an advantage, but Jess steeled herself to stay cool. She knew, from listening to Max and Bob talking, that eight competitors would run in the second heat, and four in the last, and she drew on second-hand expertise to save the stallion until the final one.

They came in seventh, although if she had let Cloud have his head Jess knew they could have done better. Nina, who made second place, jeered, 'This is no place for amateurs,' as they lined up again for the second heat.

To her relief Jess drew a place two sulkies distant from the other girl, and found herself track neighbour to the man who had bid against them for the sulky at the farm sale.

He recognised her, and called out in a surprised voice, 'Max not driving today?'

She replied, 'He's hurt his wrist.'

'Good luck,' he called back sportingly as they started off again on the second round.

Jess felt she needed all the luck she could get.

By now the crowd had latched on to the fact that the Blythe colours were in with a chance, and since Max's tall figure was clearly visible with his guests in the VIP box, that it must be Jess herself who was driving.

Some of the teenagers from the youth club, with whom she had made friends at the dance, began to cheer her on, and a crowd of locals from the other side of the stands took up their chant, and above the hard smack of hooves on the track surface, and the hum of spinning sulky wheels, a new sound assailed Jess's ears.

'Blythe...Blythe...Blythe...'

A hundred voices shouted encouragement to her. Jess's ears heard their message, but her heart listened for one voice only, and that one remained silent.

Its absence served to increase the icy coldness inside her as she sped on. With detached clarity she remembered the driving instructions she had received, never thinking for one moment that she would ever actually need them in a race.

'For the first time or two, let your horse find its own way,' Bob had cautioned her. 'The animal will know the ropes better than you do.'

Jess thrilled to find this true. Cloud seemed to sense that this was her very first race, and took it upon himself to further her instruction.

The stallion not only knew the ropes, he seemed to know the track rules as well, Jess realised, amazed. The horse saw openings she would not have dared to ask it to go through, and she caught her breath as her sulky skimmed by the wheels of her competitors with only an inch or two to spare, but never once cutting across their path, and laying her open to a charge of foul play.

He wants to win as much as I do. Cloud wants to win for Max, Jess thought jubilantly, and when they reached the home straight she simply sat still, and left the rest to the stallion.

This time they came in third, and Jess wondered with momentary panic, what if I've misjudged Cloud? And myself? What if we lose the next heat, and the horse is disgraced, and Max shamed in front of everybody?

Max would blame it on her own incompetence, and she would have no defence against that. It must be virtually unheard of for a novice to attempt a cup race, taking on some of the best international drivers.

Her confidence began to drain away, and before she could hit rock bottom she plugged the leak hastily with a stout reminder to herself, if I'm taking on the best drivers, they're taking on the best horse, and turned the sulky determinedly to line up for the last heat.

Cloud's ears were still pricked forward and he breathed easily, which justified her holding him in during the other two heats. This time Jess drew the position on the inside rail, and Nina was next to her, with the man they met at the auction taking third line, and the other competitor on the outside rail.

When they started off, the speed of the final heat took Jess's breath away. It made the previous competition look as if it had been standing still.

The second the mobile starting gate swung off the track, the horses leaned into their traces as if they knew they were racing for the cup, and believed their drivers must either win or die.

Jess thrilled to the rush of air against her face, but she felt no fear. The first two heats had given her the feel of racing, and with only four sulkies spanned out across the track, there was plenty of room on each side.

Being on the inside against the rails made the turns a little bit tighter than before, but Max had trained Cloud to every position on the track, and the stallion knew exactly what he was doing.

This time round Jess asked the horse for speed, and he gave it nobly. In no time, it seemed, the home stretch flew towards them, and two of the competitors began to lag behind.

Jess glanced round.

Nina was still with her. They were racing with their sulky wheels within a short foot of each other. Nina was a lot too close for safety, edging in to gain the advantage of the narrower circle instead of remaining, as she should have done, in her own track.

Jess called out a warning, 'Keep your distance,' and knew shock as she caught sight of the vicious expression on the other girl's face.

Leaning forward in her seat, she urged Cloud on. It was as if she and Nina were the only competitors in the race. In one respect, that was true. They were competing against one another in a personal, private race, and the prize was not a silver cup, it was a man.

The crowd shouted, 'Blythe,' but Jess's heart cried, 'Max,' and she acknowledged now that her reason for doing this was him, and not merely to teach Nina the lesson she so soundly deserved. She was not racing even for Cloud's reputation, but simply, and solely, for Max.

And because of this she had to win, or her heart would die.

Cloud flew as if he sensed her need. Out of the corner of her eye Jess saw Nina lay her whip across her horse's back, and winced for the animal, which managed to drag another ounce of speed from its blowing lungs, and remain on a level with Cloud.

No gladiators ever fought a more desperate contest. No quarter was asked and none given, and the crowd gradually ceased its chanting and grew silent, sensing, if not understanding, that higher stakes than a silver cup were being fought for in the duel taking place in front of them.

Slowly but surely Cloud's superior speed began to tell, and he drew ahead. Nina used her whip again, but this time it had no effect. Her horse had no more speed in reserve.

Nina lashed again, and screamed out loud at her animal, 'Faster, you...'

The wind carried her words away, but the horse was giving all it had and could give no more, and with a shrill cry of rage Nina wrenched hard on the nearside rein.

Jess knew stark fear as the other girl's sulky hurtled towards her. A feeling of disbelief gripped her, as it flashed across her mind, she's going to ram me into the rails!

If they crashed at this speed she could be killed. At best, the stallion would suffer terrible injuries, and Max would never forgive her for that. He would blame herself, she knew, and not Nina.

A horrified murmur rippled across the crowd, and died away into an awful, waiting silence.

Terror paralysed Jess. Her throat could not cry out to urge Cloud on. Her hands clung to the reins, like a parachute harness, Max had said, but his training held, and she remained automatically leaning forward, so that the leathers did not pull on Cloud's sensitive mouth and hold him back.

The stallion's ears were laid back now, flat against his head like a cat at bay, seeing the peril on his other side. Jess wanted to close her eyes, but did not dare. And then, across that awful gulf of waiting silence, a shout like a bugle call rang out from the stands, loud and clear and commanding.

'Go!'

The stallion's laid back ears caught his master's command, and the horse responded like clockwork. He surged forward, using every ounce of his reserve, and Jess ducked as the head of Nina's horse swerved above her, almost on top of her.

And then they were through. The blow had missed her by inches, and the crowd was on its feet, locals and strangers alike yelling, 'Blythe, Blythe, Blythe,' as they flashed across the finishing line a good couple of lengths ahead of the others.

Max presented Jess with the silver cup.

She was to have presented it herself to the winner of the race, and the surprise substitution further delighted the crowd, who applauded wildly as she reached up her hands to receive it.

They faltered as they gripped the shiny sides. The smile on Max's lips failed to reach his eyes, which were bleak and unresponsive, and dark with an anger that boded ill for when they were alone together later.

His congratulatory phrases, which read the exact opposite from his stormy glance sounded hollow in Jess's ears. Instead of letting the cup go, Max slid his fingers over her own as she took it, trapping them underneath his, and played to the crowd by bending down and kissing her hard on her lips. Exactly as everyone expected a proud husband would do.

His lips were as unyielding as his eyes, bruising her own, punishing her for what she had done. Which had been to win him the trophy and prove Cloud to the harness-racing world, but instead of being glad he hated her for it, and Jess's eyes stung so that she had to rely upon Cloud to find his own way during the obligatory victor's lap round the track with the cup, followed by the man they had met at the auction, who had won the shield of the second prizewinner.

The fourth contender had been obliged to retire with a broken trace, and Nina was disqualified for foul play. With brutal frankness it was announced over the loudspeakers that an enquiry would be held later to decide whether she should be banned from racing for the rest of that season, for a flagrant breach of safety regulations.

The victor's lap safely over, Jess drove straight off the track without looking back. The storm of applause from the stands followed her as she gained the stable yard and handed Cloud over to the ecstatic head lad before turning towards the tack-room herself to pick up her discarded hat and dress and shoes.

Reaction set in as she gathered them together, and black depression enveloped her; she tucked her clothes under her arm and felt a great weariness that made the heavy silver cup seem to drag on her other arm as she turned to go outside.

Max stood in the tack-room doorway, barring her exit.

Jess faltered to a stop and stood staring back at him dumbly. He did not speak. His face was dark and set, and he stepped inside and deliberately heeled the door shut behind him.

Another stride brought him up against her, so close that they touched, and Jess had to raise her face to look up into his. She stared at him as if mesmerised, and a thought strayed across her frozen mind.

Had Nina won, after all? In spite of everything, had Nina lost the cup, and won the prize?

Jess swallowed painfully, but no words came. Her heart beat with slow, agonising thuds that closed her throat to sound and, unable to bear the silence for a moment longer, she lifted her arm and held out the silver cup towards Max.

A stray beam of sunshine, penetrating the tack-room window, struck sparks of light from the highly polished sides. They flashed across his eyes, making him blink, and broke the spell that bound him. He reached out with both hands, but he did not take the cup.

Instead, he took Jess by the shoulders, and his fingers gripped her with a fierce strength, as if he felt an urge to shake her. Jess tensed against his hold, and his eyes bored down into her own, as he grated, 'Why did you do it? *Why?*'

Oh, that he should ask her such a question. Jess found her voice, and dodged it.

'You couldn't drive yourself,' she mumbled. 'And my initials are the same as yours. If you remember...'

'Of course I remember. I'm not likely to forget the initials of my own wife.'

My own wife... Jess closed her eyes on the pain and the mockery of it, and summoned anger to her aid when she opened them again to meet Max's furious glare.

'At least have the decency to accept the cup,' she cried. 'Don't you want it, now I've gone to the trouble of winning it for you?'

He shook her then. It was short and sharp, as if he was trying to shake something out of her, or something in; Jess was too shocked to know which.

'...the cup!' he swore fiercely. 'I don't want a silver cup. I want you.'

He wanted her. He did not love her. He only wanted her as a substitute wife. The agony became unbearable and her senses faded; she felt herself begin to sway. Weakly she tried to control it, but could not, and her heart dictated the direction, and swayed her towards Max.

His arms pulled her the rest of the way, and crushed her against him in a hold from which there was no escape. He buried his face in her hair and groaned, 'Oh, Jess, Jess, my love, my darling. You might have been killed, out there on the track.'

My love... my darling... The words were wrung out of him as if he was on the rack. Jess felt as if her senses must have truly deserted her, and she was dreaming.

She stammered disjointedly, 'But...Lucy...Nina...?'

'If I had my way, Nina would be disqualified from the tracks for life for what she tried to do to you today.'

'We were competing fairly enough, until...'

'She could never compete with you.'

He twisted her words to give them another meaning, and they started a warm glow travelling through Jess. She tried again.

'Nina was never really in the race, against Cloud.'

'She was never in the race at all, so far as I was concerned.'

Jess meant one race and Max meant another, and the glow spread and strengthened, and reflected in her eyes as she raised them to search his face, still doubtful, still unable to take it in.

'Oh, Jess,' he groaned. 'What does it take to make you understand that I love you? To make you love me?' His kisses rained down on her face, begging her to answer and remove his torment of doubt that was as great as her own. 'I've loved you from the moment I first set eyes on you, that morning you opened the door to me in London. Oh, yes, I believe in love at first sight now. It happened to me.'

He smiled, a bitter twisting of his lips in which there was no humour, only pain.

'From that moment, I knew just how right Lucy was. The love we felt for one another wasn't enough. She had the sense to see it, and thank goodness she saw it in time. I was blind, until you opened my eyes.' He held her from him, and the agony in his face twisted her heart. 'Don't you know what it's like, Jess, to love someone so much that every minute you spend away from them hurts as if it's your last minute on earth? That's how I feel about you.'

Jess knew, but her tongue could not find the words to reveal the innermost secrets of her heart. Perhaps later, but not now. Her silence forced Max on.

'When I saw you out there on the track with Cloud, I was paralysed with fear for you. For myself. I love you so much, I don't know what I would have done if any harm had come to you. I restored the sulky we got at York as a surprise for your birthday, and now I almost wish I hadn't. It tears me in two, to think of the risk you took.'

Words came to Jess to comfort him then. 'No harm came to me, thanks to you.' She managed a smile, and felt vaguely surprised at how easily it came to her lips after the agony of the last few hours. 'When you shouted, "Go" to Cloud, he accelerated as if he was jet propelled. All that I had to do was to hang on, and leave the race to him.'

'Cloud knew he was carrying my whole life with him. I'd confided in him often enough, how much I loved you.'

'You could have tried confiding in me.'

'I didn't dare, in case you didn't want to know. Hope was all I had to live on. Hope that, as time passed, you would learn to love me too, and that we would end up by being the lucky ones.'

His voice was raw with pain, and he went on with obvious difficulty, 'I forced you to marry me because I was so afraid of losing you. If you'd gone out of my life, it would have been worthless without you.'

'I thought you married me because...' Jess trailed to a halt.

'Because what?' He tipped up her face with three fingers under her chin, forcing her to meet his eyes. 'Tell me, Jess,' he demanded, as she remained silent.

'Because you just wanted a substitute bride, to save your face when Lucy jilted you. Maybe for an heir to your title.'

The words came out halting, hurting, and Max gave a muffled exclamation and stopped them with his lips.

'I care nothing for what the world thinks,' he muttered through his kisses. 'As for an heir, forget it. I own

Blythe. It doesn't own me. There are others to carry on afterwards, if necessary.'

His voice was tight with strain, as if he was having to exert immense self-control as he went on, 'Children must be born of love, Jess. The love of two people for each other. Anything else is unforgivable. When I saw the fear in your eyes on our wedding night, it made me realise what a terrible thing I'd done to you. Will you ever forgive me?'

Now Jess knew. Now she was sure, knowing what it must have cost him to hold back all these long weeks, for her sake. Unheeded, the dress and hat and shoes dropped to the tack-room floor, and the silver cup landed with a soft thud on top of them, unnoticed, too, as she raised her arms to clasp him tightly round his neck.

'Our child *will* be born of love,' she assured him softly. 'I'm not afraid any longer.'

'Jess, darling.' Incredulity and dawning hope chased shadow and shine across his suddenly working face. 'You're not just saying this because...?'

'I'm saying it because I love you. When I held the winner of the bonny baby competition in my arms...'

'You let him go in an awful hurry, as if you hated to hold him. If you don't like children, Jess, it isn't important. You're the only one who matters, or ever will, to me.'

'I love children. I want them. That's why I couldn't bear to hold the baby; it hurt so much because he wasn't mine—ours,' Jess corrected herself softly, and raised her mouth to meet the ecstasy in his lips.

A blissful age later she murmured contentedly, 'Our children will be champion drivers, too.'

'Children? In the plural?'

Max's look teased her, and shy colour warmed Jess's cheeks, but still smiling she let it rise and answered him bravely, 'Children, in the plural. An only child is a lonely child. I know, because I was one myself. The foal will have to look to its laurels,' she added mischievously. 'It's going to have a rival very soon.'

Max echoed her laughter, and then sobered. 'I had a letter from the vet this morning.'

'Did he send you the results of the post-mortem on the other foal?' Jess's face clouded. 'I really am sorry about that, Max. It was all my fault, putting the mare into the box next to Cloud. But I didn't know. You'll have to teach me to recognise the signs.'

Her words stumbled, confused, and he smiled down at her flushed face, and gently stroked her tumbled hair.

'It wasn't your fault. Nina owned up to what she had done.'

'Nina owned up?' Jess showed her disbelief, and a wry smile touched Max's lips.

'I shook the truth out of her. I must have been mad not to see what she was up to, but how could I suspect that she might go so far as to try to injure you, out there on the track? It's a good job the Vaughans have decided to move house,' he finished harshly, and answered Jess's startled look with a derisory, 'Kate wants to move to a more fashionable neighbourhood. They're going to Cheltenham, and taking Nina with them, thank goodness. I suppose she thought the race was her last chance.'

'It doesn't matter, except for the foal.' She stroked away the anger that tightened his face, and his lips softened into a smile that caressed her fingertips.

'Losing the foal had nothing at all to do with the uproar in the stable yard. According to the vet, there was a genetic imbalance that made it impossible for the little creature to survive.'

'I'm glad. I felt so guilty.'

Jess felt almost as bad about the letter she herself had received that morning from the fashion house. In halting tones she poured out the whole story, and finished thankfully, 'That doesn't matter now, either.'

'But it does matter, Jess,' Max contradicted her seriously. 'You must take up their offer. I'd feel so proud of your success. I haven't dared to ask you if you had a reply to the letter you sent to them, in case they took you away from me.'

'You knew about the letter?'

'Only the address. I saw it in Huw's post book, but as it was to a famous fashion house, it wasn't difficult to guess the rest. That's what made me such a beast to you, when Cloud let fly in the stable. I was so unsure of you, of myself, that I was madly jealous of anything that took your attention, even for a moment.'

'You were even jealous of Bob.' Jess's tone was a reproach, and Max had the grace to look abashed.

'I know that was silly.'

'It was sillier than silly. It was all Nina's fault. She tried to make something out of nothing, to her own advantage. Nothing can ever take me away from you. Not even our children.'

'We'll share them.' His circling arms were a strength and a promise, a safe anchor for their future. 'Just the same, they mustn't be allowed to submerge you as an individual. It's criminal to waste a talent like yours. If you do, it can only lead to frustration, and all I want is for you to be happy. But before we start thinking about careers and children, we'll have our honeymoon. We've waited long enough for it.' His hold on her tightened. 'Just you and me, alone together,' he exulted.

'It looks as if life is going to get very busy all of a sudden,' Jess murmured wickedly, and Max laughed.

'You won't have time to play with dolls,' he promised

'About those dolls...'

Jess told him all about the dolls. She laughed at his astonishment, and promised, 'You teach me about horses, and I'll teach you about antique dolls.'

'And we'll learn together about our children,' he murmured contentedly, and folded her close.

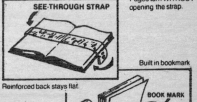

HARLEQUIN'S "BIG WIN"
SWEEPSTAKES RULES & REGULATIONS
NO PURCHASE NECESSARY TO ENTER OR RECEIVE A PRIZE

1. To enter and join the Harlequin Reader Service, scratch off the pink metallic strips on all your BIG WIN tickets #1-#6. This will reveal the values for each sweepstakes entry number, the number of free books you will receive and your free bonus gift as part of our Reader Service. If you do not wish to take advantage of our introduction to the Harlequin Reader Service but wish to enter the Sweepstakes only, scratch off the pink metallic strips on your BIG WIN tickets #1-#4 only. To enter, return your entire sheet of tickets intact. Incomplete and/or inaccurate entries are not eligible for that section or section(s) of prizes. Not responsible for mutilated or unreadable entries or inadvertent printing errors. Mechanically reproduced entries are null and void.

2. Either way your unique Sweepstakes numbers will be compared against the list of winning numbers generated at random by the computer. In the event that all prizes are not claimed, random drawings will be held from all entries received from all presentations to award all unclaimed prizes. All cash prizes are payable in U.S. funds. This is in addition to any free, surprise or mystery gifts that might be offered. The following prizes are awarded in this sweepstakes: *Grand Prize (1) $1,000,000; First Prize (1) $35,000; Second Prize (1) $10,000; Third Prize (3) $5,000; Fourth Prize (10) $1,000; Fifth Prize (25) $500; Sixth Prize (5000)$5.

   *This Sweepstakes contains a Grand Prize offering of a $1,000,000 annuity. Winner may elect to receive $25,000 a year for 40 years without interest totalling $1,000,000 or $350,000 in one cash payment. Entrants may cancel Reader Service at any time without cost or obligation to buy (see details in center insert card).

3. Extra Bonus Prize: This presentation offers two extra bonus prizes valued at $30,000 each to be awarded in a random drawing from all entries received.

4. Versions of this Sweepstakes with different graphics will be offered in other mailings or at retail outlets by Torstar Corp. and its affiliates. This promotion is being conducted under the supervision of Marden-Kane, Inc., an independent judging organization. By entering this Sweepstakes, each entrant accepts and agrees to be bound by these rules and the decisions of the judges, which shall be final and binding. Odds of winning in the random drawing are dependent upon the total number of entries received. Taxes, if any, are the sole responsibility of the winners. Prizes are non-transferable. All entries must be received by March 31, 1990. The drawing will take place on or about April 30, 1990 at the offices of Marden-Kane, Inc., Lake Success, NY.

5. This offer is open to residents of the U.S., the United Kingdom and Canada, 18 years or older except employees of Torstar Corp., its affiliates, subsidiaries, Marden-Kane, Inc. and all other agencies and persons connected with conducting this Sweepstakes. All Federal, State and local laws apply. Void wherever prohibited or restricted by law.

6. Winners will be notified by mail and may be required to execute an affidavit of eligibility and release that must be returned within 14 days after notification. Canadian winners will be required to answer a skill-testing question. Winners consent to the use of their name, photograph and/or likeness for advertising and publicity in conjunction with this and similar promotions without additional compensation.

7. For a list of our most current major prize winners, send a stamped, self-addressed envelope to: WINNERS LIST c/o MARDEN-KANE, INC., P.O. BOX 701, SAYREVILLE, NJ 08871.

If Sweepstakes entry form is missing, please print your name and address on a 3" × 5" piece of plain paper and send to:

In the U.S.	In Canada
Harlequin's "BIG WIN" Sweepstakes	Harlequin's "BIG WIN" Sweepstakes
901 Fuhrmann Blvd.	P.O. Box 609
Box 1867	Fort Erie, Ontario
Buffalo, NY 14269-1867	L2A 5X3

© 1989 Harlequin Enterprises Limited   Printed in the U.S.A.

LTY-H119

Wonderful, luxurious gifts can be yours with proofs-of-purchase from any specially marked "Indulge A Little" Harlequin or Silhouette book with the Offer Certificate properly completed, plus a check or money order (do not send cash) to cover postage and handling payable to Harlequin/Silhouette "Indulge A Little, Give A Lot" Offer. We will send you the specified gift.

Mail-in-Offer

OFFER CERTIFICATE

Item:	A. Collector's Doll	B. Soaps in a Basket	C. Potpourri Sachet	D. Scented Hangers
# of Proofs-of-Purchase	18	12	6	4
Postage & Handling	$3.25	$2.75	$2.25	$2.00
Check One				

Name _____

Address _____ Apt. # _____

City _____ State _____ Zip _____

ONE PROOF OF PURCHASE

To collect your free gift by mail you must include the necessary number of proofs-of-purchase plus postage and handling with offer certificate.

HR-2

Harlequin®/Silhouette®

Mail this certificate, designated number of proofs-of-purchase and check or money order for postage and handling to:

INDULGE A LITTLE
P.O. Box 9055
Buffalo, N.Y. 14269-9055